NELSON MALONE
MEETS THE MAN FROM
MUSH-NUT

Author LOUISE HAWES says, "Nelson's adventures are the sort of daydreams all children have and most grown-ups remember. I wrote these stories for my son and daughter, who know what's good for them and laughed at every one!"

The author lives in Ridgewood, New Jersey, with her children, Robin and Marc. This is her first book.

BERT DODSON has illustrated many books for young people, including *The Trouble With Diamonds* by Scott Corbett. He lives in Bradford, Vermont.

NELSON MALONE MEETS THE MAN FROM MUSH-NUT

LOUISE HAWES

Illustrated by Bert Dodson

AN AVON CAMELOT BOOK

AVON BOOKS
A division of
The Hearst Corporation
105 Madison Avenue
New York, New York 10016

First Avon Camelot Printing: May 1988

CAMELOT TRADEMARK REG. U.S. PAT. OFF. AND IN OTHER COUNTRIES, MARCA
REGISTRADA, HECHO EN U.S.A.

Printed in the U.S.A.

OPM   10 9 8 7 6 5 4 3 2

to Isabel and Maurice
with love

Contents

Samantha

Nelson Malone decided he'd rather grow another freckle or help his sister with her homework than take Horatio to Pet Day again.

"Horatio," insisted his mother, "is an upstanding hermit crab, a credit to his species."

"He's not bad for a crab, I guess," Nelson admitted. "But why can't I have a *real* pet?" He thought about the parrot that Shane McCallister was bringing to Pet Day. Not counting the swear word that always made Mrs. McCallister cover its cage, the big green bird knew how to say six different things, including "Relax, buster" and "Says who?"

"You know very well," said Mrs. Malone, who was not looking at Nelson, "that your father is allergic to fur." She was staring intently at a small machine on the table in front of her. It had lots of red and green

1

buttons and a transparent top through which Nelson could see tiny wheels and gears. "Welcome to the wonderful world of your new E-Z prune pitter," his mother announced.

"But the whole fifth grade has already *seen* Horatio. I've taken him to Pet Day for three years in a row." Nelson wanted action, not pitted prunes. Mrs. Malone looked up and nodded, then reached for one of the pencils she always kept behind her ear. She started writing very fast on a piece of paper.

"Mom," Nelson tried again, "you can't win first prize by falling into your water bowl, and let's face it, that's Horatio's best trick."

But it was too late. Mrs. Malone was already at work. "Maybe," she said out loud to herself, "it would be better if I started with a question instead." She crumpled the sheet of paper she'd been writing on into a ball, stared at a new sheet, and asked in a bright, cheery voice, "Tired of pitting prunes, peaches, and dates by hand?"

Nelson's mother usually worked in her office at the E-Z Can Opener Company. She sat behind an army-colored desk and wrote instructions for all the kitchen tools that E-Z made. On the front of her desk, right next to the picture of Nelson and his sister Robin, was a big gold sign with black letters. E-Z, the sign read. BECAUSE YOU'VE GOT SOMETHING BETTER TO DO.

"Horatio doesn't even have teeth," Nelson complained. "If he at least had teeth, he could do neat stuff like Eric's dog." If Nelson's mother hadn't been working at home this week, he could have called her at the office. She always listened when he phoned her.

2

He could have told her how, even though Pet Day was still a week away, he was already tired of hearing all the kids at Upper Valley Station Elementary boast about their pets.

Especially his best friend, Eric Lerner. Every time Nelson rode his bike to Eric's house, his friend's huge, shaggy dog bounded across the yard carrying an egg clamped in his teeth. Eric always waited until the dog had stopped running and stood patiently in front of the boys. Then he would raise his hands high and scream, "Smash it, Woton!"

The last time Eric and Woton had practiced their new trick, Nelson couldn't help being impressed. First Eric threw the egg to Woton, who caught it in his mouth then rolled over and over until Eric gave the command. "Wow!" Nelson told Eric while Woton licked sticky yolk from his whiskers. "That was awesome." Woton stopped licking the yolk and started licking Nelson's hand. "My dad says he used to have a cat that cracked walnuts. But that was before he became allergic to feathers, fur, and anchovies." Woton began sniffing Nelson's high tops all over, as if his nose were a metal detector and something very valuable were hidden in Nelson's sneakers. "Now Dad can't even get near my sister's tiny mouse without sneezing."

"You mean," asked Eric, "you've never had a smart pet like Woton?"

"Not unless you count Maurice," said Nelson, feeling very sorry for himself. "Maurice was my Venus's-flytrap. In second grade, I taught him how to eat grilled cheese sandwiches."

"Wow!" It was Eric's turn to be impressed.

"He was pretty neat," said Nelson. He sighed as if he were remembering an old friend. "Then one day he ate my strawberry-iced Ding-Ring Date-Nut bar, shriveled up, and snapped closed forever."

"Gosh, Nelson. I'm sorry," said Eric, hugging Woton tightly.

As Pet Day drew closer, Nelson decided drastic measures were called for if he was going to be able to take anything besides a hermit crab or a goldfish to school. That was why he decided to make the bet with Robin. "You have more freckles than I do," he told his sister on the way home from school one day.

"Do not, dumbhead," answered Robin, who was just as blonde and every bit as full of freckles as her older brother.

"Do so." Nelson was waiting for the right moment. Then he saw his sister make her stubborn, lemon-tasting face. "Betcha," he said quickly.

"I'll bet you a hundred, million, trillion dollars." Even though she was only in the fourth grade, Robin was very confident.

"How about your white mouse against my hermit crab?" asked Nelson, trying his best to sound as if he had just thought of the idea.

But it was no good. Robin shrieked as if Nelson had suggested selling her entire Day-Glo shoelace collection. "I'd never trade Rinaldo for that stupid old crab!" The pink pom-poms on her ponytails shook with indignation. "Besides, I'm taking him to Pet Day again. Maybe he can win first prize twice in a row."

"Ratty Rinaldo," Nelson told his sister, "only won

last year because he spilled my model paints all over himself the day before the show." He remembered how long it had taken to scrub his rug clean and how he'd decided to leave the spot under his desk because, unless you were a midget or crawled into the room on your hands and knees, you couldn't see it. "Who wouldn't give a prize to a mouse with #168 silver ears and a #203 camouflage green tail?"

"Mom says Rinaldo has noble features," Robin insisted. "I think he would have won even without the accident. You could paint that smelly old crab of yours with glow-in-the-dark polka dots, and he'd look like a loser anyway. So if you think I'd bet my lovable, prize-winning mouse against your boring, never-won-a-thing-in-his-life hermit crab, you're crazy. And you *still* have more freckles."

Nelson had run out of ideas. He had also run out of #3 phosphorescent purple and #16 pulsating pink, so painting Horatio's shell, even though it was a pretty good plan, probably wasn't the answer. (After checking his pockets for leftover allowance to buy new paints, he decided it *definitely* wasn't the answer.) That's when he remembered the stickers Mrs. Pauley, his piano teacher, always gave him after each lesson.

Every Thursday for as long as he could recall, Nelson Malone had walked to Mrs. Pauley's house after school. He would play songs like "Trot Along, My Pony" or "Laughing Brook" while the heavy little woman clapped her hands and chanted in time to the music, "Lis-ten, Nel-son, lis-ten to the beat." Then she would purse her lips, lick a sticker, and paste it beside his next assignment. Nelson always buried his music

5

book at the bottom of his backpack so none of the guys at school would see the yellow smiley faces and silver stars on every page.

But now it occurred to him that silver stars could give Horatio a crucial competitive edge against talking parrots and egg-cracking dogs. And smiley faces might be just the thing to bring out the personality Nelson's pet kept hidden under his drab brown shell. With two or three of the tiny, bright stickers on his back, Horatio could crawl his way to victory!

Mrs. Pauley was very surprised to find Nelson Malone at her door. Some of her students occasionally stopped by to chat, and one or two of the little ones visited her for extra help, but Nelson was the last student she would have expected to be enthusiastic about piano.

"Come in, Nelson," she said, looking confused. "Are you locked out? Is it time to order Christmas cards already?"

Nelson studied his piano teacher's face. Mrs. Pauley was quite fat, and she looked as if she had joined the Wart-of-the-Month Club as soon as she was born. But she was always smiling, and he decided she might understand about Horatio. So he explained his problem and asked her for some new, unlicked stickers from the sheet she kept on top of the piano.

But Mrs. Pauley shook her head. "I'm afraid that's not in Horatio's best interest, dear," she told Nelson. "How do you know he doesn't breathe through his little shell? Can't you take another animal?"

"My dad is allergic to other animals," Nelson told

6

her. "Besides, Pet Day is tomorrow. Horatio's my only hope."

"Perhaps not," Mrs. Pauley said. She looked suddenly thoughtful, leaning her double chin on a chubby hand. "Just what is it your father's allergic to?"

"Anchovies, feathers, and fur."

"In that case," announced Mrs. Pauley, "I think Samantha can help."

"Who?" asked Nelson.

"Not that she'll want to," continued Mrs. Pauley, grabbing Nelson by the hand and leading him into her kitchen. "She's never very cooperative. Have a cookie." His piano teacher scooped two Peanut Crunchies from a jar on the counter and then opened the basement door. "Follow me," she said, munching her cookie as she led the way downstairs.

"You understand this is just between us, Nelson. Strictly top secret." When they reached the bottom of the stairs, she opened a small door with a gold key that was hanging from a chain around her neck. "So there's no need to tell your mother and father about my laboratory." She pushed open the door, and Nelson followed her into a small, dark room. "After all, I've only been at this a couple of years now, so I'm not really very good yet."

"Good at what?" asked Nelson, peering into the gloomy corners of the room as Mrs. Pauley lit a candle.

"At witching, dear." His teacher walked past a table filled with pots and glass jars to a large box at the back of the room. It was draped with black cloth embroidered with shiny silver writing that Nelson couldn't read.

Nelson noticed a strange, familiar smell, like burnt matches. "What's witching?" he asked, swallowing his peanut cookie hard.

"Why, witching, the art of being a witch." Mrs. Pauley laughed. "Of course I don't really qualify yet. I suppose you'd have to call me an apprentice witch. A very junior grade witch, Samantha always says. Don't you, Samantha?"

"Sssssso what if I do?" hissed a voice from the box under the black cloth. Nelson took several steps backward and knocked over an old broom that had been propped against the wall. Leaning it quickly back into place, he watched his piano teacher pull the cloth cover from the box and found himself staring into the yellow eyes of the longest, fattest snake he had ever seen.

"This is Samantha, dear," said Mrs. Pauley, reaching one of her fat, braceleted arms into the box and patting the gray green coils. "She's my familiar."

His last bite of cookie still made a hard lump in the middle of Nelson's throat. "Your what?" he asked, coughing hoarsely.

"My spirit-helper," replied Mrs. Pauley as the snake raised her head from the box and began to uncurl. "Oh, I know. I know. Witches' helpers are supposed to be black cats. But after all, I'm new at this, and I had to take what I could get."

"Sssssecond-rate witches need firssst-rate familiars," hissed Samantha, flicking her long pink tongue next to Mrs. Pauley's ear.

"I suppose you're right, Sammy." Nelson's teacher sounded rather discouraged. "It's just that I do wish you weren't always so critical. I'm doing the best I know how."

"Precisssssssely the problem." The snake sneered. "The bessst you know is the worssst I've ssseen." She turned and trained her steady yellow gaze directly on Nelson. "Assss for you," she told him, "I'll need three glasses of water and a dish of ground bat's toes every day."

"Bat's toes?" Nelson had backed into the broom again but steadied it without taking his eyes off the giant snake. He could hardly believe he was in the same house where he'd practiced "Climbing the C Scale" since he was four years old.

"Yesssss," Samantha hissed irritably. "You *are* taking me to Pet Day, aren't you?"

Even before she had raised her big, scaled head close to his, her tongue darting in and out, Nelson decided he would probably do anything Samantha wanted. "It would be an honor, ma'am," he said quickly.

"Oh, how marvelous, Sammy!" Mrs. Pauley clapped her hands and looked quite pleased with herself. "I wasn't sure you'd want to go. I thought you might make a fuss about leaving me on my own."

Now that Samantha was stretched full-length in front of him, Nelson was astounded to find that she was at least twice as long as he was tall. He imagined what his parents would say if he brought her home with him. "On the other hand, ma'am," he told her, "if you don't *want* to come to Pet Day, that's really, perfectly, completely all right."

The snake ignored Nelson and turned her head to glare fiercely at Mrs. Pauley. "Sssssylvia," she hissed, "*you* are not ready for ssssolo ssssstudy, but *I* am ready for a sssssabbatical."

"Sabbatical?" asked Mrs. Pauley. "What do you mean?"

"I mean," said Samantha, snuggling up to one of Mrs. Pauley's glass jars, "I'm going on vacation. Your training has been very hard on me. Amateurs are alwaysss difficult, and I've shed three ssssskins nursssssing you through Basic Witchcraft." She wrapped the end of her tail around the glass and shook the cloudy yellow liquid inside it. "I just don't think," she added more softly, "that I have the ssstrength to sssee you through Intermediate Broom Travel or Potions II."

"But Sammy, dear," protested Mrs. Pauley, "I've made such good progress lately." Nelson's teacher seemed bent on convincing Samantha she was trustworthy. "Why, I've only set my hat on fire once this month—and I got yesterday's spell nearly right."

"Turning that toad into a piece of fruit may be your idea of nearly right," said the snake, putting the glass jar down and shaking her great head. "But the spell called for a *prince,* not a *quince.*"

"They sound so much alike." Mrs. Pauley pouted. "How was I to know?"

Nelson thought about all the witch stories he'd ever heard. They were always about expert, wicked witches, but he supposed even the best of them must

11

have been beginners once. "Maybe you could turn the quince back into a toad and start over," he offered.

"It only proves," Samantha continued, ignoring Nelson again, "that you can't be left alone. That's why I'm going to find you a ssssubstitute familiar at Pet Day. Then I'm going to take a nice long sssssiesta in a cool, deep hole." The snake swayed back and forth, her hiss low and steady. "I'll choose a fat, furry dog or cat to clean up your messses and correct your misssstakes. I've had it."

"You mean you'd take somebody's pet away from them?" asked Nelson, more worried than ever. What if Samantha chose Woton? How could he ever explain *that* to Eric?

"Sssskinny boy," hissed Samantha, "leave everything to me. Jussst let me ride home in your pocket and it will all work out for the best, trussssst me."

Nelson looked at Samantha, who had to be the largest snake in the world. Even though he had stretched his pocket by filling it with convertible robot parts and an orange tennis ball from the racquet club he walked past on his way home from school, there was not the slightest chance of Samantha fitting inside.

"Ma'am, I just don't think—" he began. "I mean, even though I'd like to, I'm pretty sure you'd be much too heavy. Nothing personal, ma'am."

But Mrs. Pauley's familiar was not listening. Instead, she slithered once again toward the glass jar, while his music teacher pried open the lid. Then the snake flicked her long tongue into the yellow liquid, and Nelson watched an incredible change take place.

Samantha seemed to shrivel up in an instant, and before the jar was drained, she had turned into a tiny green snake just like the ones Nelson used to find under rocks by the water sprinkler in his backyard.

"Now, Nelson," said a small, quiet voice he could barely hear, "put me in your pocket."

Although it was difficult to believe the sweet little whisper came from Samantha, Nelson did as he was told. After the tiny snake was curled safely in his pocket, and after he had promised Mrs. Pauley three times that he would never mention her "hobby" to anyone, Nelson hurried home.

The next day was Pet Day. In the morning, Nelson, who was anxious to stop at Mrs. Pauley's house for some bat's toes, insisted he didn't want any breakfast before school.

"But Nelson," Mrs. Malone told him, "I've made waffles, and we have a new box of Bronco Puffs."

"Eleven years old," announced Nelson, "is too old for cereal that's shaped like pink and green cowboy hats."

"You won't be eleven for three weeks," Robin said, using her last piece of waffle to soak up her last drop of syrup. Her six pink plastic bracelets made tiny clicking noises as she whirled her fork around her plate.

"All right, space mouth," Nelson told his sister, "if you're such a whiz at figuring, maybe you can figure out how I'm supposed to eat breakfast and help set up Pet Day at the same time!"

"Which reminds me," interrupted Nelson's father, who had already eaten his waffle and was folding the newspaper into neat little squares like a napkin, "where's Horatio? Doesn't he usually go to Pet Day with you?" He finished folding the paper and put it into his briefcase.

"I'm not taking Horatio this year, Dad," said Nelson.

"That's too bad." Nelson's father sounded genuinely disappointed. "Horatio has never made me sneeze, unlike certain rodents who shall remain nameless," he said, looking straight at Robin. "Besides, I thought Horatio was sort of a tradition at Pet Day."

"A losing tradition," observed Robin, standing up to take her plate into the kitchen and spilling a giant glob of syrup onto the cover of Nelson's social studies book. "Excuse me, I have to go comb Rinaldo's tail."

"Aa-a-choooo!" said Mr. Malone, thinking of Rinaldo's tail.

"Sssssss," said a small voice from inside Nelson's pocket.

"What, Nelson?" asked Mr. Malone.

"Ssssss," Samantha repeated. Nelson watched the syrup glob spread over the first few letters of the book's title, until *Discovering Our World* turned into *covering Our World*.

"Ssssyrup will do nicely," hissed Samantha a bit more loudly.

"I thought you weren't eating, dear," said Nelson's mother, putting a waffle on his empty plate and passing him the bottle of maple syrup. "Actually I can't blame you. I'm afraid it's time to update the manual for the E-Z waffle iron. I followed my directions exactly, but this last batch tastes more like garden gloves than waffles."

Nelson shifted uneasily in his seat as the faint voice came again from his pocket. "They're better than bat's toes," said Samantha.

Nelson's father looked very surprised. "Nelson Malone," he said sternly, "is that any way to talk to your mother?"

Quickly Nelson broke off a tiny piece of his waffle and stuffed it into his pocket. But Samantha wasn't finished. "Of coursssse," she added thoughtfully, "ssssalamander's eyes are better than both."

"Nelson," said Mrs. Malone, sounding a bit hurt. "They *are* tough and leathery, but garden gloves is as far as I'm willing to go!"

"Don't talk with your mouth full," Nelson whispered sharply into his pocket.

"Lissssten, freckle face," hissed the little snake, "ssstop throwing your weight around."

"Leave the table at once," ordered Mr. Malone. "And don't come back until you can behave like a human."

"I'd rather be a three-toed ssssloth," said Samantha as Nelson wiped the cover of his social studies book. As quickly as he could, he jammed the book, his lunch, and three sticks of Nifty-Bubble into his backpack, kissed his parents, and ran out the door.

The gymnasium of Upper Valley Station Elementary was crowded with cages, boxes, and baskets. The big room echoed with chirps and barks and twitters. It wasn't only students, Nelson noticed, who had brought their pets to school. Mr. Dabber, the gym teacher, was standing beside his stubby little bulldog, Butch; Mrs. Ferigno, the art teacher, had brought Mittens, her Siamese cat; and even the principal, Mr. Glendinny, had come with some kind of animal—although no one could tell what it was, because he kept it covered in a small blue box with air holes in the top.

"Hi, Nelson. Where's Horatio?" asked Eric. He was bent over Woton, trying to untie a big pink ribbon from the dog's left ear. "Can you help me get this dumb bow off Woton? Mom says it gives him pizzazz, but I think it's giving him an earache."

"I decided not to bring Horatio," said Nelson, backing away from Woton, who began sniffing at his pocket with more than a little interest. The dog's metal-detector nose was wiggling furiously, and his big, wet tongue was tickling Nelson underneath his New Jersey Generals football shirt.

"Sssssscram, horse breath," hissed Samantha loudly.

Woton and Eric looked very surprised.

"What?" said Eric.

"Woof," said Woton.

"Get losssst," said Samantha from Nelson's pocket.

"Boy, just because your father's allergic to pets," Eric told Nelson, "doesn't mean you have to take it out on us!"

"I'm not," insisted Nelson, very tired of taking the blame for Samantha. "Here, I'll give you a hand with that bow. It does look pretty silly." Together he and Eric finally untangled the pink ribbon; then Nelson decided it was time to have a boy-to-snake talk with Samantha.

"Did you come to Pet Day to pick a new helper for Mrs. Pauley," he asked the snake in the boys' room, "or did you just want to make my life miserable?"

Samantha poked her head out of Nelson's pocket and blinked at the light. "At leasssst," she said indignantly, "you could have taken me to the girlssss' room."

"I could *not*," Nelson told her, "unless you really want to start trouble! Now listen, I think you'd better choose a witch's assistant fast, so we can get out of here before I lose every friend I have."

"Not until I win firssst prize."

"You mean you actually want to *enter*?"

"Of course."

Nelson knew he'd better act fast. He had just decided to twist his pocket closed with a rubber band when the small green snake suddenly crawled up his shirt buttons and began swaying rhythmically, like a charmed cobra, just under his chin. She closed her scaly eyes and hissed a soft, musical chant.

"What are you doing?" gasped Nelson, feeling the snake suddenly growing heavier on his shoulders.

"Sssstretching," replied Samantha, and she certainly was. Within minutes the tiny snake curled around his neck had returned to the size she'd been in Mrs. Pauley's laboratory. Her huge coils wrapped around him like a muffler, so that Nelson felt very warm and very nervous. "Jusssst tell them," the giant snake hissed, "that I'm a present from your uncle in Africa."

"But I haven't *got* an uncle in Africa," protested Nelson, taking a deep breath and opening the bathroom door.

Not counting the two boys who broke out in hives and the one teacher who fainted, Samantha was the unanimous choice for First Prize Pet at the Upper Valley Station Pet Day. She stayed coiled around Nelson's shoulders and darted her long tongue in and out without saying a word. Everyone was very impressed.

"Your uncle in Africa must be very proud," Mr. Glendinny told Nelson as he presented him with a silver trophy and, standing far back from the giant snake, let Samantha wiggle her long body around a big blue ribbon.

As the principal prepared to award the second-place ribbon to his own long-haired hamster, who had been a real crowd pleaser ever since she'd eaten the top off her blue box, someone pushed her way to the front of the crowd around Nelson and Samantha.

"We don't *have* an uncle in Africa," Robin told everyone. She was carrying a tiny cage in which Rinaldo was busy turning his exercise wheel. Even though he'd just lost his chance to win twice in a row, the little mouse looked a lot happier than Nelson's sister.

"Have you ever *been* to Africa?" Nelson asked, grinning broadly.

"Of course not, warp brain," answered Robin, hugging Rinaldo's cage to her chest and edging cautiously toward Samantha.

"Then how do you know we don't have an uncle there?" As Nelson spoke, Samantha unwrapped herself from his shoulders, flicking her huge tongue close to the Popsicle-shaped barrettes in Robin's hair.

"Your mousssse," she hissed so softly that only Robin could hear, "lookssss delicioussss."

Robin screeched and dropped Rinaldo's cage on the gym floor. The mouse, who had fallen off his exercise wheel, eyed her reproachfully and then began to lick his long, thin tail.

Robin pushed her way through the children holding dogs on leashes and cats in their arms. Only when she reached the heavy exit door did she turn to look back at Samantha and Nelson. "Just wait," she yelled to them from across the gymnasium, "till you bring that overgrown worm home. You'll be sorry!"

Nelson felt Samantha's coils unwrap from around his neck again, but this time he was ready. He grabbed the tip of her huge tail just in time to prevent her from slithering down his arm. "Please," he urged, tugging at Samantha's tail like a rope until he had retrieved two of her coils, "we still have work to do. You've got to find Mrs. Pauley's assistant." He was very glad no one else had heard the snake speak to Robin, and he was anxious to return her to his piano teacher without any more trouble.

But Samantha, wriggling furiously to escape Nelson's grasp, looked very much like more trouble. "Overgrown worm?" She hissed, still fighting to ooze out of Nelson's arms onto the floor. "Did she sssay overgrown worm? Why, I'll turn that ssskinny sssister of yours into a rat, a bat, a microbe." The snake was so large and was twisting and turning so fast that Nelson could hardly hold her. "I'll make her invissssible. I'll give her horns on her head, moles on her nossse and hivesss everywhere!"

Even though there were times when Nelson, too, would have liked to have made his sister invisible, he couldn't help remembering how she usually let him have all her lemon Life Savers and how she never told their father who threw the Frisbee through the garage window. "Robin didn't really mean any harm," he told Samantha. "She just talks a lot faster than she thinks."

Nelson was afraid that someone might overhear Samantha's grumbling, but the children around him were so busy yelling and pushing one another in an effort to touch the big snake that he could hardly hear a sound.

"Congratulations, Malone," said James Frackey, the biggest boy and the second-best fighter in the fifth grade. "That's some snake."

"It's not so hot," said Darcy Staples, the biggest girl and the best fighter in the fifth grade.

"Sssss," hissed Samantha, watching Robin, who still stood, hands on her hips, by the big gym door.

"Snakes have no brains," continued Darcy, "just like you."

"SSSSSS," hissed Samantha so loudly that Darcy backed into Mr. Glendinny, who was pinning the third-prize ribbon on Shane McCallister's parrot's cage. Darcy, the principal, and the parrot cage tumbled in a heap to the floor.

"Watch your step, Miss Staples," said Mr. Glendinny, brushing birdseed off his trousers.

"You'll pay for this, Malone," promised Darcy as she helped the principal to his feet. "Wait till I get my hands on you at recess tomorrow."

"Relax, buster," said Shane's parrot.

Once Darcy and Robin had stormed out of the gym,

Samantha began to settle down. She was curled like a large emerald collar around Nelson's neck when his friend found them.

"Hi," said Eric. "I brought Woton over to shake paws." Samantha glared at the big, shaggy dog and hissed sharply. But Woton seemed to think she was being friendly. He wagged his tail eagerly and put his big, wet nose right next to hers.

"Thanks, Eric," said Nelson. "I'm sorry Woton dropped the egg."

"Oh, that's OK," said Eric. "Your snake would have won anyway. That's the biggest, best, and most exciting pet I've ever seen. Where did you get it?"

Nelson thought about his promise to Mrs. Pauley. "I just borrowed her from a friend," he told Eric. "I have to take her back after school."

"Gee, that's too bad," said Eric, looking longingly at Samantha, while Woton tried to lick the tip of her gently swaying tail.

"Oh, it's all right," answered Nelson. "I've always got Horatio."

Only after Samantha had shrunk herself to pocket-size again and they were on their way back to Mrs. Pauley's did Nelson remember to ask. "Well, ma'am," he said into his pocket, "what about a new familiar? We didn't find one."

"Yesssss, we did," the tiny snake answered in her thin voice. "You're bringing him over tomorrow."

Nelson thought of all the pets he'd seen that day. But he couldn't imagine any of them as Mrs. Pauley's witching assistant. Not even the cats seemed to have

Samantha's intelligence or courage. "Who is it?" he asked his pocket. "Who did you choose?"

"Horatio, of course," came the reply. "He and I had a long talk last night, and he's agreed to fill in for me for a few months."

Nelson couldn't believe his ears. "Horatio? But he's just a hermit crab!" He thought of the dumb way Horatio was always trying to climb up the glass sides of his terrarium and falling backward, legs waving, onto his shell. "He's so small and quiet, and . . ."

"Persssssistent," finished Samantha. "Horatio is devoted, determined, and very trussssstworthy." The tiny snake peered from Nelson's trousers. "And," she added, "he could teach *you* a thing or two."

Nelson thought of how often he had forgotten to fill Horatio's water bowl and how many times his mother had fussed at him for letting the terrarium get dirty. "Do you think," he ventured shyly, "that before he goes, Horatio could teach me how to make Darcy Staples disappear?"

"I wouldn't be sssurprised," hissed Samantha softly. "I wouldn't be at all ssssurprised."

Baby-Thinks-All-Day

Piano lessons were a lot less boring after Horatio moved in with Mrs. Pauley. Although Nelson told his family that he had lent the tiny crab to Eric for a science project, Horatio was actually hard at work in Mrs. Pauley's laboratory. As soon as Samantha left for her vacation, Nelson's piano teacher and her new familiar started research on an automatic broom pilot. Nelson really couldn't see that they were making much progress since neither of them ever left the ground. But at least he got to eat cookies in the basement instead of practicing scales in the living room.

Every Thursday Nelson came home with a bag of cookies and a new silver star or smiley face. He felt a bit guilty about the stickers. After all, he wasn't really playing piano assignments for Mrs. Pauley anymore. His teacher, however, insisted on sending the shiny shapes home with him. "Your talent," she told Nelson, "does not lie in the realm of music, but that doesn't mean it shouldn't be rewarded. You are the only student I've ever had who could eat more cookies than I do."

At first Nelson had no idea what to do with Mrs. Pauley's stickers. Then he realized that they would make a perfect welcome-home gift for Horatio. He began to paste the little shapes on his absent pet's terrarium. Pretty soon the empty glass bowl under his bed started to look as cluttered and colorful and comfortable as Nelson's own room. Just the sort of place, Nelson decided, where a fellow could put up all ten feet and relax!

Nelson liked clutter. His room was littered with friendly, reassuring souvenirs. He never threw anything out because everything was worth saving, and he never kept things where they belonged because everything belonged anywhere. One day Nelson's father brought home a big green sign shaped like a trash can. It had black letters across the top that said GARBAGE DUMP. "Harry Taylor kept this on his desk at the office," Mr. Malone told Nelson. "Harry's desk is the *second* worst mess I've ever seen." Nelson liked the funny sign just as much as he liked his comfortable, messy room. He thanked his father, wrote STAY OUT under GARBAGE DUMP, and taped the trash can on his door.

But someone couldn't read. Because one Thursday Nelson Malone came home to a neat room! Not only had someone made his bed, thrown out his thirteen empty Tangerine Bubble-Lite bottles, and undone the paper-clip chain between his bed and desk, but that same someone had also scrubbed every single sticker off Horatio's bowl!

"How could you?" he asked his mother. "My collection of broken model parts was almost big enough to make a robot, my football cards are out of order, and Horatio's bowl is covered with big sticky spots where you peeled off all his silver stars!"

Nelson's mother, who was dripping yellow batter all over the stove and who had stopped vacuuming his room once the pile of Galactic Vampire figures was high enough to cover the electrical outlet, smiled mysteriously. "I'm not the one who's growing up and cleaning up by leaps and bounds," she told him. "You'll have to discuss your room with your sister." She put two muffin tins into the oven, forgetting to wipe up the round yellow drips that were already puffing up like tiny dollhouse muffins on the hot stove. "Personally I was just learning my way around up there. The last time I put laundry in your drawers, I made it all the way to your dresser without tripping over anything!"

"How could you?" Nelson asked Robin, who was busy arranging her schoolbooks in alphabetical order by the authors' names. "You threw out all my Mush-Nut bar wrappers, and I only needed forty-three more to get the Whammo Magic Kit, including the trick of the disappearing dime!"

Robin Malone was only nine years old, but she folded her arms and looked at Nelson as if he were a naughty child and she were his teacher who'd asked him to stay after school. "I simply couldn't *stand* it anymore," she told her big brother. She wrinkled her nose the way people do when they smell something awful. "Your room was a disgrace. It made too much work for Mom and me. And believe me," she added, wrapping all her yellow crayons together with a rubber band and putting them in her desk beside three more crayon bundles—one red, one green, and one made up of all the colors there weren't enough to make bundles of—"we have enough to do around here."

"Since when are *you* so perfect?" demanded Nelson. He knew for a fact that Robin always left the top off Monopoly and usually stuck her old Bammo bubble gum under the roof of her dollhouse. "You're not my mother. What gives you the right to go around making other people's beds?"

"Perhaps you'll understand when you're older," answered Robin, sounding far away. She didn't even call him "dumbhead" or "weirdo." Nelson felt very strange.

"Perhaps *you'll* understand when someone cleans *you* out." Nelson stamped over to his sister's shelves, determined to show her how it felt to lose your past. But he couldn't. Robin's shelves were empty! There were no old teddy bears leaking beads of stuffing and no droopy-eared dogs. "What happened?" he asked, too amazed to be angry anymore. "Did you throw away all your toys?"

"Of course not," said Robin, sounding more distant and grown-up than ever. "It's just that I don't need silly playthings now. Mom said I could send them to our new baby cousin in Ohio." She showed Nelson a huge cardboard box in her closet, already full of soft, furry animals, coloring books, and Smell and Tell storybooks. "The only trouble," she complained, "is that you can't trust anyone under three with moving parts, so I have no one to give these childish toys to."

Nelson could hardly believe what he saw. Robin had gathered all her dolls together and stuffed them into a pillowcase. A big Candy Cupcake and a smiling Baby-Drinks-All-Day were nearly falling out of the bulging sack.

"You mean you're not going to be a kid anymore?" Nelson asked, very surprised and more than a little worried about the change in his sister. *One* mother was all right, but the last thing Nelson Malone needed was two people telling him to chew slowly and put the cap on his glue! "You love dolls," he insisted. "You begged Mom to get you Baby-Drinks-All-Day just this summer. You can't throw away a brand-new toy!"

"Well, *you* take her then. I don't have any use for her." Robin pulled the plastic baby from the pillow-case and, without even looking at its fat, cheery face, threw the toy at Nelson's feet. When the doll hit the ground, the round button on her back was depressed and the rejected toy squeaked, "Mama, hug me."

"You're crazy!" said Nelson, scooping up the little doll. "Why don't you like her anymore?" He remembered the cardboard high chair Robin had made for Baby-Drinks-All-Day. He remembered that every night she put her favorite toy to sleep on top of all the other toys on her shelf—even the fancily dressed foreign dolls.

Robin sighed the way their mother did when she

looked at old school pictures of herself in the photo album. "You know, Nelson, I can't stay a little girl forever. Warren Lansdorf says I look and act like a seventh grader."

"Warren Lansdorf is only in fifth grade, so how would he know?" Nelson thought about the way creepy Warren was always making spit rockets that missed the lunchroom aide by a mile. "Besides, he's just about the biggest gorfhead in the whole school. And believe me, I can tell, because I have to sit next to him for library and music."

"Warren says I'm very mature for my age," Robin continued in a voice that sounded as if she hadn't played with dolls in years. "He gave me a bracelet with a stopwatch that almost works."

There was no talking her out of it. If Warren Lansdorf thought she was grown-up, that was good enough for Robin. The pillowcase of dolls got wedged under the basement stairs and Baby-Drinks-All-Day ended up on Nelson's workbench, where he tried desperately to think of something he could make with all her pink plastic parts. Nelson was very good at taking things apart and almost as good at putting them back together. He was certain he could invent something startling and revolutionary using the doll's rolling eyes and maybe the long plastic drinking tube he found curled inside her neck.

But a spanking clean room was no help when it came to inventing. Robin had thrown out all his useful odds and ends—his collection of rusted springs from broken ball-point pens, his assortment of watch straps and belt buckles, even his pile of chain from an old backyard swing. Clearly Nelson needed inspiration and spare parts.

For three days Nelson Malone hammered and sawed at his workbench. For three days he refused to tell Robin or his mother or father what he was working on. Finally, when his best friend asked him what he was inventing, Nelson had to admit the truth. "I don't know," he told Eric Lerner. "Everyone keeps asking me, but I really don't know. I've taken apart my Mr. Math calculator, and I thought I might try to use these wires to make Baby-Drinks-All-Day a very smart doll."

Eric, who lived only two streets from Nelson and who traded lunches with him when Nelson's mother put onions in his sandwich, tried to help. But he wasn't used to inventing things or to girls' toys. He stared at the shiny, pink baby from whose back all the Mr. Math wires spilled like curly spaghetti. "Well," he laughed, "if you make a smart doll, ask her to do my homework, will you?"

Nelson knew that Miss Benito, the fifth-grade teacher, had already had a conference with Eric's mother about his long division. He also knew a good idea when he heard one.

"That's it!" he told Eric, thumping Baby-Drinks-All-Day on her diapered bottom. "That's it; that's what I'll invent!" He shook Eric's hand the way he had seen Orville shake Wilbur's in a movie about the Wright brothers. Wilbur was just kind of talking away when all of a sudden he gave his brother an idea about how to get their plane off the ground. "A homework machine!" shouted Nelson, connecting his calculator to the doll's drinking tube. "Think of the time it will save! Why, we can solve problems without ever doing them! We'll play Monsters and Miracles while Baby-Drinks-All-Day does our homework!"

"*Thinks*-All-Day," said a small, squeaky voice from the workbench. Nelson and Eric stared at the plastic doll lying facedown on the bench. Then they looked at each other.

"Baby-Thinks-All-Day," said the muffled voice again, "not Drinks-All-Day." The wires running between Mr. Math and the plastic doll made the calculator's lights blink with every word. "I'm not a drinking doll anymore. Now I'm a thinking doll, and I think I'd like to turn over."

Eric stood very still. His mouth and eyes opened wide until they looked like the O shapes on a cartoon face. Nelson, who was pretty surprised by his own invention, reached down cautiously and turned Baby-Thinks-All-Day onto her back.

Now that they could see her face, Nelson and Eric were amazed to find the doll's eyes and mouth moving as she talked. "It took you long enough to figure me out," she said, rolling her blue marble eyes toward Nelson. "I thought you'd never finish." Her voice sounded stiff and high, like a whirring cake mixer.

"I didn't even know what you were going to be," explained Nelson. "I'm usually a pretty fast inventor."

"Well, now that I'm invented, what would you like me to think about?" Baby-Thinks-All-Day asked. "I need something to take my mind off that unpleasant sister of yours."

"You mean Robin?" Nelson moved the tangle of

tools and toy parts off the top of his workbench to give the doll more room. She was moving her plastic arms and legs in a silly, useless pattern the way a turtle does when it's turned over on its shell.

"I mean that nasty, ungrateful girl who decided to dump me before a single spring had snapped or a single part had worn out." Baby-Thinks-All-Day finally succeeded in raising herself on her chubby elbows and turned to face the two boys. "I mean that cruel child who pretended to be my mother, fed me with a pink Raggedy Ann spoon, and then threw me out like old garbage!"

Even though teasing Robin was almost as much fun as tripping fat Hildy Crosser, Nelson felt funny listening to someone else complain about his sister. "She didn't really mean it," he told the doll. "She's just a dumb girl, and you can't expect her to act reasonable. Besides, you won't see her anymore. I'm going to have to hide you from the whole family if you're as smart as I hope you are! First let's see if you can do my homework."

Nelson dashed upstairs to get his school notebook, leaving Eric alone with Baby-Thinks-All-Day. Eric studied the tiny doll carefully. Suddenly, as if he were trying to catch her by surprise, he yelled, "What's 283 divided by 116?"

"Calculating to the nearest hundredth, 2.44," replied the toy rather huffily. "Don't you have something more interesting? How about quantum physics? Or even a quadratic equation?"

"Wow!" Eric was impressed but not entirely convinced. He started to walk away from the workbench,

32

then turned sharply, pointing a finger at the pink doll. "OK, Miss Know-It-All, what's the capital of Uruguay?"

"Montevideo, pea brain," squeaked the doll.

When Nelson returned with his notebook, he found Eric scribbling furiously on a pad. "Nelson." Eric looked up at his friend with an expression of joy very much like the smile he'd worn the day he'd gotten his silver and green dirt bike. "She's done *all* my long division. She knows *everything!*"

"Of course I do," said the tiny toy. "After all, I think all day. Mostly about that mean old Robin."

"Forget about Robin," said Nelson. "You'll have plenty of other things to think about from now on! You're not a silly old baby doll anymore. You're my brand-new, top secret, one-of-a-kind homework machine!"

Nelson took his homework machine to school every day. He hid the doll in his desk and propped the top open with a fat blue eraser. All week long, Baby-Thinks-All-Day lay between a science book called *How High the Stars?* and a pile of old test papers marked "careless," "pay attention," or "try harder." From inside Nelson's desk, she whispered the answers to all of Miss Benito's questions, and every day Nelson got a star for having the best test scores in his class. Now Nelson's hand was always the first up when the teacher asked a question. Now Miss Benito always called on him when there were visitors in the room. "Nelson," she told everyone, "has made great strides."

Each day Nelson and Eric carefully smuggled Baby-

Thinks-All-Day out to the playground at recess. They hid her in a book bag and carried her out to third base on the baseball field. In five minutes the doll did both boys' homework. When they got home, Eric and Nelson had nothing to do but play. Nelson had a lot more time to spend with Mrs. Pauley and Horatio. He even had time to build a new, record-breaking paper-clip chain from his bed to his desk to his closet to his chair to the bathroom door.

"What is *that*?" asked Mr. Malone, tripping over the chain on the way to his morning shower.

"Creative problem solving," announced Mrs. Malone, who was convinced that the curling string of clips was responsible for Nelson's new math prowess. "He doesn't even need to use paper and pencil anymore."

At the end of two weeks, Miss Benito called Nelson's mother to tell her how much his schoolwork was improving. At the end of three weeks, she called to make sure Mrs. Malone was sending the right boy to school. "I can't believe the change in your Nelson," she gushed into the phone. "I just want you to know that, even though a teacher's job can sometimes be exhausting and discouraging, it is minor miracles like this that make me know I'm really helping."

Miss Benito was so happy that Nelson was almost as upset for her as for himself when Baby-Thinks-All-Day started making mistakes. At first, they were just little errors, like dividing when she should have multiplied. Soon, though, it was apparent that Nelson's homework machine needed a major overhaul. "What is the capital of Argentina?" Miss Benito asked her class.

Baby-Thinks-All-Day squeaked her answer from inside Nelson's desk, and without thinking, Nelson raised his hand and repeated, "Thirteen hours and fifty-six minutes."

Nelson thought new batteries might help. He used his whole week's allowance to buy four new Ever-charge C-cells. But, even though her eyes rolled and her plastic arms moved and the calculator wires hummed, Baby-Thinks-All-Day seemed to have lost her brainpower.

"If John starts at three o'clock and Harry starts at four," Miss Benito asked the fifth grade, "how long will it take them to cut the grass?"

Nelson's hand shot up and, before he could stop himself, he had repeated after the doll, "Martin Luther King." Miss Benito looked very confused.

Not only was Baby-Thinks-All-Day forgetting how to think, she was beginning to act more and more like her old baby-doll self. One day she refused to do Nelson's homework until he agreed to put her in her old high chair and give her a drink from Robin's play baby bottle. The next day she told Eric that 4,369 divided by 922 was one mama!

"What's the matter with your homework machine?" Eric asked Nelson after school one day. He had ridden over to Nelson's house to show him the latest note Miss Benito had written his mother about long division. Mrs. Lerner had not looked happy when she read it. "I thought that doll was supposed to know everything."

"She does," insisted Nelson, "but I think she'd rather be a baby doll than a homework machine." He offered Eric half a chocolate chip cookie and helped him park his dirt bike by the porch. "She still wants to play house and do girl stuff with my goofy sister."

They went down to the basement where Baby-Thinks-All-Day sat stiffly in her old high chair. "What about quadratic equations?" Eric asked the doll, staring fiercely at the Raggedy Ann spoon on the tray in front of her. "What about capitals? And what about long division?" He plucked the plastic baby from the chair and sat her on the couch beside his books. "Look, Baby-Whoever-You-Are, you're really making things hard on me! Miss Benito is sending notes to my mother again. You better stop eating and start thinking!"

"I'm tired of thinking," the squeaky voice answered him. The doll's blue eyes rolled in her head, and she fell over on her side. "No one puts me to bed at night. No one changes my dress. No one hugs me since that awful Robin threw me away and turned me into a machine."

"She did not!" Nelson interrupted. "*I* turned you into a machine. But I'm an inventor, not a baby-sitter. And if you think I'm going to play house with you, you don't know so much after all!"

"*I'll* play house with you," Eric volunteered. "I'll change your dress, and you can even sleep under my bed with Woton. He's a good dog and his bites don't really hurt." He scooped the doll from the couch and started to carry her upstairs. "Just help me pass the math test tomorrow so Miss Benito and my mom will stop seeing so much of each other. They're already calling each other by their first names!"

Before Baby-Thinks-All-Day had a chance to consider Eric's offer, Nelson rejected it. "No way, Eric," he said, grabbing the doll from his friend's hands. "You may be my best friend, but I built this homework machine, and I'm not letting you take her."

"But I gave you the idea for building her, didn't I?" asked Eric, yanking Baby-Thinks-All-Day back.

"I made her all by myself on *my* workbench," yelled Nelson, tugging at the doll's leg and trying to pull her away from Eric. "I used *my* tools and *my* brains, and you'll be sorry if you try to steal *my* invention!"

"Oh, yeah?" challenged Eric, pulling the doll's other leg.

"Yeah," huffed Nelson, twisting one of Baby-Thinks-All-Day's arms out of Eric's grasp.

"Mama!" wailed the miserable toy as she was snatched and pulled in two different directions.

"Grr," growled Nelson, pulling his side of the doll harder than ever.

"Rrrrr," roared Eric, tugging on his side so furiously that he sent Nelson sprawling, still clutching a pink arm and leg.

"Now look what you've done!" said Nelson, dismayed at the tangle of doll parts lying on the floor.

"I don't want your old homework machine anyway," announced Eric. He threw his side of the toy on the ground, stormed up the steps, and rode home.

Surveying what was left of his invention, Nelson decided to operate. If he put Baby-Thinks-All-Day back together again, maybe he could fix whatever had been making her act so queerly. Maybe, if he started all over at his workbench, he could make her *more* calculator and *less* baby doll. The one thing he hadn't counted on, however, was Robin catching him at work.

"What are you doing to my doll?" his sister screamed when she saw the pink arms and legs spread across Nelson's bench. "Look what you've done to my favorite doll!" Her eyes were shiny and full of tears. "Who said you could ruin my toys, dumbhead?"

"*Your* toys?" Nelson wondered what had happened to his mature, elegant sister who didn't need dolls. She hadn't even mentioned how messy his workbench was! "You gave this stupid doll to me, knucklehead. Remember? What would Warren Lansdorf say if he knew you were making such a fuss over a baby toy?"

"Warren Lansdorf is gross." Robin came closer, studying the scattered pieces of Baby-Drinks-All-Day. "All he cares about is looking at bugs. He even puts dead beetles in his lunch box. He asked me for his dumb stopwatch back so he could give it to yucky Brenda Lawson. When I wouldn't give it to him, he gave me an Indian burn." Nelson noticed that his sister's voice sounded small and shaky, as if she were trying not to cry.

"I told you he was a creep." Nelson kept working while he talked. "I also told you that you shouldn't throw away a brand-new toy." He stuffed the doll's arms back into her body and plugged in the Mr. Math wires. Even though it meant revealing his secret invention, Nelson decided it was time to show Robin the wonderful change he'd made in her discarded toy. "Luckily for you, I've improved Baby-Drinks-All-Day. She's now the smartest doll in the world. Watch."

The calculator lights blinked on and off, and the doll's marble eyes rolled. Nelson took a deep breath and picked up the toy. "Baby-Thinks-All-Day," he asked in a slow, even voice, "what is 94 times 3,248?" Suddenly the blue eyes stopped turning and focused on Nelson's sister. The doll raised her dimpled arms high and answered, "Mama, hug me."

"Oh, Nelson," squealed Robin. "You were right!" She scooped the doll into her arms and hugged her as if she were a real baby. "She *is* the smartest doll in the world. She knew I didn't really want to throw her out." Robin carried Baby-Drinks-All-Day, calculator wires trailing behind her, to the old high chair. "You stay right here," she told the doll. Next she took the pillowcase from under the stairs and emptied all her old dolls onto the couch. She examined each one carefully, then covered them all with a fuzzy wool blanket. "There," she said, "there's nothing wrong with any of my toys. And there's nothing wrong with a fourth grader liking dolls, either."

"I guess you're right," Nelson agreed, unplugging the Mr. Math wires from Baby-Drinks-All-Day. He was quite relieved to see Robin acting like a nine-year-old and to have only one mother again. Besides, a good inventor could definitely use a bracelet with a stopwatch that almost worked to build a new, improved, maintenance-free homework machine. "You have more freckles than I do," he said, bending over his bench.

"Do not," answered Robin, holding her doll very tight.

"Betcha," Nelson said, grinning broadly.

"I'll bet you a hundred, million, trillion dollars!"

"How about Warren Lansdorf's watch against my 747 mechanical pencil with retractable landing gear?"

"How about my knuckles against your nose, fuzz ball?" Her brother was very quiet, and Robin was very puzzled. She couldn't figure out why Nelson kept smiling at her, but then she didn't know how good it felt to get your kid sister back!

Mohammed
El-Janrez

By the time Samantha's sabbatical was over and Horatio was ready to come home, Robin had stopped tidying up and Nelson had saved enough stickers to turn the crab's terrarium into a wonderful hodge-podge of yellow smiley faces, silver stars, and black eighth notes with glossy tails. The little crab scratched a silver star off his bowl with one sharp claw, mixed the shiny sprinkles in his food, and then settled down to being a perfectly ordinary hermit crab. He was as quiet as ever, and he fell into his water bowl just as often as before, but Nelson was very glad to have his pet back at last.

Horatio's new home, however, seemed to upset Mrs. Malone. "I feel so guilty," she told him, studying the hermit crab's colorful bowl. "You've redecorated Horatio's room, and he's only three years old." She placed her hands on Nelson's shoulders and stared at him earnestly. "Here I've let you turn eleven without lifting a tape measure."

His mother's eyes were shining the way they had just before she put the chandelier in the bathroom. "What do you mean?" Nelson asked her, not at all sure he wanted to know.

"It's just that you've outgrown your surroundings." She marched to his bed and picked up the spread. "No wonder you never make your bed. You've got teddy bears dancing all over your bedspread!" She let the spread fall and began pacing the room, her arms folded. "You need a new look, Nelson—something forceful, something sporty, something . . ."

"Teddy bears?" asked Nelson. "Dancing? I thought they were tin soldiers marching."

Nelson's mother stopped pacing and bent over his bed. "No," she said, examining the little blue silhouettes very closely. "No, they're definitely teddy bears, and they definitely have to go."

And they did. Several weeks after his birthday, a very tall woman from Grochman's department store redecorated Nelson's room. She covered his bed in a color she called "rugged red," and his curtains were buckskin beige with little rugged red basketball players running all over them. If you squinted your eyes, they looked just like the teddy bears that used to run all over his old bedspread, but Nelson decided not to mention it.

Fortunately the tall woman also chose a new rug for his room. This meant Nelson had to clean under his bed, and that meant he found some things that even

Robin had missed when she stripped him of his past. Armed with a flashlight and his mother's warning that the men from Grochman's had better not find anything but his old carpet under the bed, Nelson crawled under the dust ruffle.

He came out with some useful items he'd forgotten about. Besides a lot of rubber bands and the missing *W* from his old Scrabble set, Nelson found the big ball of string he'd started rolling in first grade, three Star Fight bubble gum cards, and a library book that was due two years ago. He also found his old basketball uniform. The shorts were gray with a black stripe, and the jersey had a big number 14 on the front and TROTTERS written in black letters on the back. Nelson had played only one game last season before he'd been "sidelined with an injury," which meant he had spent all winter in a tight, sweaty cast watching his team play without him. When he found his uniform, Nelson decided that things would be a lot different *this* year.

The day before basketball tryouts, Nelson put on the uniform in front of his mirror. It was a little tight, but he could still imagine himself leading the Upper Valley Station Trotters to victory—dazzling his opponents with his savvy and speed, scoring basket after basket, and remaining quiet and humble, like Space Spy just before he zaps an enemy with his light beam.

The day after basketball tryouts, Nelson started eating beets. No one expected him to eat anything besides mashed potatoes, french fries, and cheeseburgers without catsup. His mother had given up asking him to "try just one bite" of things several years ago. So when Nelson asked for a second helping of beets at dinner, his family was very surprised.

"Beets contain iron," he explained in between bites. "Mrs. Woolsey, our health teacher, says iron fosters growth." He made an awful medicine face and then swallowed hard. "How much growth do you think these beets could foster by Thursday, Mom?"

Nelson's mother wasn't sure. Neither was his father. "Why do you need to be bigger by Thursday?" asked Mr. Malone, passing the silver beet dish to Robin, who shut her eyes tight and pushed it to the other end of the table.

"Because," Nelson told him, "I'm the next-to-the-shortest kid on my basketball team. Our first game is Thursday, and if I don't get taller fast, fat Hildy Crosser is going to play center." He glared at the last beet on his plate. "She's only in the fourth grade, but she's a lot bigger than I am."

"And a lot *better*, too!" added Robin. "You should see her play kickball at recess! A lot of the boys tease her and call her 'fatface' and 'two-ton,' but none of them can kick as far as she can."

"None of them have as much behind their kicks," said Nelson, hiding his last beet under his mashed potatoes and wondering what Hildy Crosser fostered *her* growth with.

"She's got a lot more going for her than weight," insisted Nelson's sister. "She's in my gym class, and Mr. Dabber says she's the finest natural athlete he's ever seen."

"Gee, motor mouth, that's great," snapped Nelson. "Maybe you and Mr. Dabber should start a Hildy

Crosser fan club. Besides," he added, stabbing his last beet through the mashed potatoes, "if I hadn't been in a dumb ankle cast all last winter, I'd be just as good as Old Three Chins."

"If you hadn't tried to do a popper-wheelie over Mr. Sheean's rosebush, you wouldn't have missed a whole basketball season, gobhead."

Nelson's mother cleared her throat and smiled a huge, phony grin like their principal, Mr. Glendinny, at an assembly. "Well, gobhead and motor mouth," she said, "thank you for expressing your views. And now, if you don't mind, I think we can bring this discussion to a close."

But Nelson was remembering how uncomfortable the cast had been. He remembered watching the other boys on the team, and wishing like anything that Mr. Sheean's rosebush had been a lot smaller. "All I know," he announced stubbornly, "is that Hildy Crosser has dimples on her dimples, and she doesn't even know who Mohammed El-Janrez is."

He thought about the way Hildy had stolen the ball from him at tryouts. He thought about the way she had dribbled circles around him when he tried to guard her. He wished like anything that *she'd* been a lot smaller, too!

"If a dumb fourth-grade girl who doesn't know who the most famous basketball player in the world is beats me out," he said, standing suddenly to carry his plate to the kitchen, "I'll quit the team!"

"That's poor sportsmanship," announced Robin as Nelson, without saying "Excuse me," left the table and stormed upstairs to his room.

"That's poor table manners," his father called up to him as Nelson slammed his door so hard that his *Revenge of the Brain Eaters* poster fell on the floor.

Nelson picked up the poster and turned on the weather-station alarm-clock pencil-sharpener radio he had earned by selling greeting cards to everyone who lived between Norwood Avenue and Edward Place. Then he sat on his bed and sulked. Somehow tryouts had not been the triumph he had planned. For a whole year Nelson had waited to play basketball. He'd dreamed of dancing downcourt with the ball as his teammates cheered and of soaring through the air toward the basket the way Mohammed El-Janrez did on TV. Instead Nelson had found the distance from the ground to the huge orange hoop was a lot farther than he had counted on. Instead each time he dribbled, the ball ran away from him, refusing to jump back to his hand the way it did for Mohammed.

"Don't worry," his friend Eric had told him after tryouts. "This is your first year playing basketball. You just need more experience." Then Eric patted him on the shoulder as if he were years older than Nelson. "Heck, Nelson, you should have seen *me* at the beginning of last season. I was almost as rotten as you are!" That was when Nelson had decided to eat beets.

"DO YOU THINK YOU HAVE TWO LEFT FEET?" A big, deep voice on the radio startled Nelson, who was trying to figure out why his foul shots always rolled backward between his legs. "ARE YOU COMING IN LAST," the voice on the radio asked him, "IN THE RACE FOR STAMINA AND STAYING POWER?"

Nelson nodded vigorously and listened closely now

to the low, familiar voice. "THIS IS MOHAMMED EL-JANREZ, LITTLE BUDDY, AND EVEN THOUGH YOU MAY NOT BE SIX FOOT TEN LIKE ME, I WANT TO HELP YOU WIN THAT RACE."

"Wow!" said Nelson, surprised that the famous basketball star knew about his tryouts. "Mohammed El-Janrez, if I could play like you. If I . . ."

"YOU MAY NOT BE THE NATION'S LEADING SCORER LIKE I AM," Mohammed interrupted him, "BUT YOU CAN SCORE BIG POINTS WITH SUPER ALL-SPORTS SNEAKERS."

"You mean my old sneaks are no good?" Nelson asked. "I got them at Michael Payjack's father's shoe store, and Mr. Payjack told Mom the heels are reinforced like radial tires."

"YOU KNOW," Mohammed continued, "YOU MAY NOT BE THE KLUTZ YOU THINK YOU ARE."

"Yes, I am," insisted Nelson. "Didn't you see me miss that pass from Eric?"

"IT COULD JUST BE YOU'VE BEEN WEARING THE WRONG ATHLETIC SHOE. LITTLE BUDDY, DON'T YOU WANT TO BE ABLE TO COUNT ON YOUR SHOES WHEN YOU'RE IN A TIGHT SPOT?"

"Well," admitted Nelson, "I *did* trip on my laces right after Hildy Crosser stole the ball from me."

"YOU BET," answered Mohammed, as if he were talking just to Nelson. "THAT'S WHY I WANT YOU TO RACE DOWNCOURT TO YOUR NEAREST SHOE DEALER AND TELL THOSE FOLKS YOU WANT TO JOIN MOHAMMED EL-JANREZ'S WINNING TEAM."

"I will! I will!" yelled Nelson.

"WHEN YOU SIGN THE ALL-SPORTS ROSTER, YOU'LL

BE GETTING A LOT MORE THAN A PAIR OF SHOES, LIT-
TLE BUDDY."

"I will? I will?" asked Nelson.

"YOU'LL BE GAINING SKILLS AND CONFIDENCE YOU
NEVER KNEW YOU HAD. SO GET MEAN, JOIN THE ALL-
SPORTS TEAM!"

"You bet, Mohammed. But can I ask you one thing?
Remember when I wrote you that long letter last winter?"

"THIS IS YOUR FRIEND, MOHAMMED EL-JANREZ,
SAYING . . ."

"Don't you remember? I sent you a Band-Aid so you
could autograph it and I could wear it on my ankle
cast?"

". . . BE A CHAMP, NOT A CHUMP. . . ."

"How come you never answered me?"

"SO LONG, TEAMMATE."

Maybe the Band-Aid got stuck to my letter, thought
Nelson as the basketball star's voice faded and music
began to play. Or maybe I forgot to use my zip code.
His favorite rock group, Slam, was playing their big
hit, "Tears in My Burger," but Nelson was too excited
to listen. He turned off his weather-station alarm-clock
pencil-sharpener radio and thought about money.

The situation was desperate. He had already spent
his entire week's allowance on six packages of green
Zonkers and a Gruesome sticker that looked exactly
like a drop of blood when he put it on on his notebook
cover. Even if he asked for next week's allowance
early, he wouldn't have enough money to buy a
brand-new pair of sneakers. Even if he gave up his
allowance for a whole month, he couldn't afford to

join Mohammed El-Janrez's winning team! If he were
to add all the leaf-raking money he'd been saving in
his secret drawer to buy a model submarine with re-
movable crew and torpedoes, there still wouldn't be
enough for a pair of Super All-Sports. Nelson knew
there was only one thing to do.

"I'll let you play my Slam album whenever you
want," he offered Robin. "You don't even have to
ask." Robin crossed her arms, shook her head, and
made her lemon-tasting face.

"All right, then." Nelson groaned. "If you lend me
the allowance money you've saved, you can keep the
album and my record player in your room until I pay
you back."

Robin's eyes widened, but she didn't uncross her
arms or stop shaking her head. "No deal, dumbhead,"
she said firmly.

Nelson pictured the new high tops and all the
power and stamina they would give him. He couldn't
bear to spend this basketball season watching games
from the bench—not after he'd spent last season
watching them from the bleachers. "OK, OK," he
conceded. "You can have the album and the player in
your room—and I'll be your slave for a week."

Robin uncrossed her arms. "A month," she insisted,
smiling wickedly.

Nelson felt his pride crumbling, but he had to draw
the line somewhere. He put his hands on his hips and
tried to sound like his father talking about responsibility and character. "Two weeks," he growled, "and not
a second more."

It worked. Robin shook his hand instead of her

50

head. "Two weeks," she shrieked, "and no backsies!" She took her old blue clown bank down from its shelf and unscrewed the stopper on its bottom. Out fell more dollar bills and quarters and dimes than Nelson had ever seen together in one place. Robin handed him all her change and ten of the bills, then stuffed the rest of the money back into her bank. "Mom says it's going to rain tomorrow, slave," she announced grandly, "so I think I'll ride your bike to school."

After school the next day, Nelson walked in the rain to Michael Payjack's father's shoe store. "Goodness, young man," said Michael's mother when she saw him. "Where's your raincoat?"

Nelson tried not to drip on the shoes as he searched the rows and rows of sneakers for a pair with the familiar red Super All-Sports star. "My sister's wearing it," he told Mrs. Payjack. He saw high-top Panthers with suede inserts. He saw sporty Nigels with vented air holes. But he didn't see a pair of All-Sports anywhere.

"My," said his classmate's mother, "I wish Michael were as considerate of Elsa. I'll bet your sister is pleased as punch to have you for a brother!"

"She sure likes it better now than she will in two weeks," answered Nelson, remembering how Robin had made him put his dessert in her lunch box before they left for school. He was beginning to think Payjack's didn't carry All-Sports, when his eye caught the huge cardboard figure at the back of the store. It was a life-size cutout of Mohammed El-Janrez, all six feet ten inches of him! The tall, dark basketball player was smiling and holding out his hands toward Nelson. Holes were cut into the display so that the famous star appeared to be carrying two shoe boxes. Piled around the base of the figure were more shoe boxes, all stamped with the bright red All-Sports star.

"Can I have a pair of those, please?" asked Nelson, pointing eagerly to the display.

"Only if you like peppermint pink, Nelson." Mrs. Payjack smiled apologetically, then opened one of the boxes at Mohammed's feet. Inside was a pair of brand-new canvas high tops with rubber soles and the red Super All-Sports insignia on the heels. "You see," she explained, "the All-Sports company made a mistake and sent us a whole shipment of the same color. Unfortunately, it isn't a very popular shade."

Nelson could understand why. The shoes in the box were a vivid, candy pink. With the red stars and bright red laces, they looked a lot more like a strawberry sundae than the super sneakers he had been waiting for! He patted the pocket where his leaf-raking money and Robin's "bank" loan were hiding. Then he thought of how the kids on his team would laugh if they saw him in pink sneaks.

Nelson didn't want to believe that every box in the display contained shoes of the same ridiculous color. He opened box after box, only to find pair after pair of shocking pink All-Sports. Finally he reached for the last box in Mohammed's hands. "LITTLE BUDDY," he seemed to hear the deep, gentle voice again. "I KNOW YOU WANT TO BE ABLE TO COUNT ON YOUR SHOES WHEN YOU'RE IN A TIGHT SPOT. RIGHT?"

"Right," admitted Nelson. "But maybe two left feet are better than two pink ones!"

"I don't blame you," said Mrs. Payjack. "Michael says he'd rather clean up his room every day for the rest of his life than wear these sneakers." She closed the shoe boxes and placed them back under the display. "Mr. Payjack has already phoned the All-Sports people, and they're coming to pick up the shoes tomorrow. We'll get our money back, but we can't get any more All-Sports in until next season."

"You mean," asked Nelson miserably, "it's strawberry or nothing?"

"Oh, no," Mrs. Payjack reassured him. "We carry lots of other fine shoes. How about a pair of Silver Streaks? Their heels are reinforced just like radial tires."

"I know," answered Nelson. "But they won't put me on Mohammed El-Janrez's winning team." He stared at the cardboard figure's smiling face. "They won't help me win the race for stamina and staying power." He still held the box he had taken from Mohammed's hands. "What size are these?"

"Why, they're size four," Mrs. Payjack told him. She took the box from him and began to walk with it back to the All-Sports display.

"I thought so," said Nelson. He could hear all of Upper Valley Station laughing as he told the surprised woman, "I'll take them."

Mrs. Payjack took Nelson's money and handed him the box with the red star. "Well," she ventured, "at least you'll know no one else in town has a pair of sneakers like yours."

Nelson took a last look at Mohammed, who now held only one pair of Super All-Sports. He was still smiling right at Nelson. "YOU'LL BE GAINING SKILLS AND CONFIDENCE YOU NEVER KNEW YOU HAD," he seemed to promise. As Nelson left the store, he hoped that it was true. It was a little risky, trusting someone who hadn't returned your Band-Aid.

When he got home, Nelson smuggled the shoe box up to his room as if he were a spy transporting top secret documents. If Robin caught him and commanded him to do her homework, he'd never have time to get ready for the Upper Valley Station Trotters' first game.

He opened the box on his bed, carefully lifting the new sneakers from the crackling tissue. Their pink canvas sides fairly glowed, and their red laces lit up the room. All his hopes for the season depended on these strange, candy-colored shoes, and suddenly Nelson was in no hurry to put them to the test. Slowly he packed the empty shoe box with his crayons, magic markers, and two space-shuttle erasers. Next he found some freshly laundered sports socks in his dresser drawer, and finally he placed the super sneakers on his feet.

They felt like nothing he'd ever worn. Laced tightly, they hugged his ankles and sent a tiny charge of energy up through his body. Cautiously Nelson edged toward his mirror and peered at his pink feet. They looked just as awful as he had been sure they would. But suddenly something incredible happened. Nelson rocked back on his heels and posed like a basketball player taking a jump shot. Then he gave a little hop. Before he could stop himself, the pink shoes soared up past the top of the mirror, and Nelson hit his head on the lamp that hung from his ceiling!

It was several minutes before Nelson dared to try another jump. This time, as before, his feet seemed to propel him like rockets, and he felt himself leaping effortlessly across his bed and landing in the wastebasket by his desk! As he repeated these experiments, he found that he could control his powerful sneakers better and better. Soon he was bounding with dazzling dexterity toward imaginary baskets and changing directions with a blazing speed that enabled him to move toward two different corners of the room before he'd even caught sight of himself in the glass.

Nelson could hardly believe how easily and rapidly his new sneakers maneuvered every jump and twist. After an hour, he stood panting in the middle of his room, convinced that, pink or not, the super sneaks would be on his feet for tomorrow's game. Carefully he removed the Super All-Sports and placed them under his bed, where they shone gently like a nightlight. Later, as he fell asleep, Nelson thought of Hildy Crosser. He hummed softly to himself, basking in the comforting glow of his new shoes. Just let Old Three Chins try to beat me out *now*, he thought. She'll be sorry she ever tangled with Mohammed El-Malone!

The next morning Nelson wore his super sneakers to school, and by afternoon, his patience was wearing thin. Everyone who noticed his new shoes had something to say. And everyone noticed.

"Hey, Malone," yelled the crossing guard, "your

feet look good enough to eat!" Nelson didn't answer; he just smiled and thought of the game.

James Frackey, who sat behind Nelson in class, laughed so hard he swallowed a stick of gum. "Bozo," he whispered in Nelson's ear while Miss Benito was passing out work sheets, "where'd you get the funny clown shoes?"

Nelson had wanted to turn around and invite James to meet him at recess to get a clown *face,* complete with a big red nose and a black eye! But he didn't, partly because Miss Benito had already caught him talking in class twice that day, and partly because James was the second-best fighter in the fifth grade.

Even his best friend couldn't resist making fun of Nelson's sneakers. "Those shoes are stunning," cooed Eric, prancing up and down the lunch line like a ballerina. "I hope you're wearing them to the game. We need a cheerleader!"

Nelson didn't grin, but he did bear it. Even during warm-ups, while all his teammates, except Hildy Crosser, teased him about his pinkorrific feet, Nelson managed to stay calm and humble, the way Clark Kent always does just before he turns into Superman and makes mashed potatoes out of the bullies. After all, no matter how strange his new high tops looked, he was certain they would help him outdribble, outrun, and outshoot anyone in the Valley County Junior Basketball League.

"Hey, Twinkle Toes," yelled David Waldwick, "can I have this dance?" David was the only Trotter who was skinnier and shorter than Nelson, but his voice was about ten feet tall! Soon everyone on the team, except Hildy, was calling Nelson "Twinkle Toes." He wondered if Hildy had guessed that his sneaks were special, or if she just liked pink.

"You shouldn't call people names," the heavy girl scolded David. "What's so great about looking like everybody else, anyway?" Her face got very red, and she looked pretty mad, but she didn't call David "Shrimpo" the way the others always did.

The Trotters' first opponents were a tough team from Glenview, the Weasels. Mr. Liggit, the Trotter coach, had seen Nelson play at tryouts. He did not start Nelson at center; he did not start him at guard. In fact, Nelson watched the first three quarters of the season opener from the bench while Hildy Crosser played the position he had hoped to prove himself in. He finally got a chance, though, when Eric, flushed and puffing, asked for a rest. Eric played forward, and his backup, Clinton Lewis, had the flu. The score was 20 to 8, and even Hildy had been stopped. She had managed to steal the ball only once, so Mr. Liggit, resigned to losing their first game, sent Nelson in at forward. Hildy winked at Nelson as he rushed onto the floor. "Good luck," she gasped, bracing herself for the inbounds pass.

Suddenly the Weasels broke into hysterical laughter. Screaming and clutching their stomachs, the opposing players pointed at Nelson and his Day-Glo feet. The pink super sneakers tickled the Weasels' funny bones, just as they had made everyone in school laugh all day long. Even the referee snickered into his whistle, but finally called for play to resume.

At first no one on his team would pass the ball to Nelson. They had all seen tryouts too. At last David Waldwick missed a pass to Hildy and threw the ball to Nelson by mistake. As his hands closed around the basketball, Nelson Malone felt the strange and wonderful power surge up from his feet. Before anyone could stop him, he had dribbled past all five opposing players and was within shooting range of the basket!

Nelson looked around the gym. As he stood under the orange hoop, everyone was hushed and quiet, and no one seemed to care that his feet were strawberry pink. With a single gigantic leap, like the ones he had practiced in his room, Nelson reached the rim of the basket and dunked the ball into the net. "Pinch me, quick!" he heard Mr. Liggit say, and then the applause started. Everyone in the gym, except the Weasels, was clapping wildly. Hildy Crosser, still red-faced and flushed, clapped hardest of all. "That's showing them, Nelson!" she yelled, a big grin covering her face. She might be fat, Nelson thought as he raced back to the bench for a time out, but she sure is a good sport.

For the rest of the quarter, Nelson replaced Hildy at center while she took his place on the bench. When the game was over, the Trotters had won, 24 to 20. The referee had stopped the game three times to see if Nelson had springs in his shoes, and Nelson's coach had spent most of the time shaking his head. "My boy," said Mr. Liggit as the whole team gathered around Nelson, "in all my years of coaching, I've never seen such an improvement." He shook Nelson's hand hard and then locked him in a huge bear hug. "I never dreamed the few little pointers I gave you at tryouts would pay such dividends. You are the fastest learner in the world, my boy." He released Nelson to shake his head once more. "And I am the finest coach."

After that, Nelson started every game at center, and though Hildy Crosser was only a sub, she never complained or seemed to mind that she was no longer the team's star. In fact, it was Hildy who helped Nelson win his biggest victory of the season. The Upper Valley Station Trotters' fourth game was against the High Steppers, an older, more experienced team, and everyone, including Nelson, was worried. On the day of the game, the boys and Hildy sat quietly on their bench, as ten of the biggest, fiercest-looking players they had ever seen filed into the gymnasium.

"Gosh!" Eric whispered to his best friend. "Doesn't that skinny one look like he has fangs?"

"They *all* look like trouble to me," groaned Nelson. "Coach says the High Steppers have already slaughtered the Bouncers, annihilated the Court Kings, and demolished the Fearsome Five!"

"It's true," moaned Mr. Liggit, holding his head in his hands and peeking at the High Steppers from between his fingers. "After thirty-five years of coaching, I'm going to lose my first chance to go undefeated!"

"Wow!" Hildy whistled and folded her hands in her lap. "I sure am glad *I'm* not starting at center!"

"The way you can steal the ball, Crosser," Nelson said, "I wish we were *both* starting out there."

The coach took his head out of his hands and brightened. "Why not?" he asked. "Hildy, I'm starting you at left forward today. Whenever you get the ball, hand it off to Nelson."

"Yes, sir," answered Hildy. "I'll do my best." And she did! No matter how the High Steppers' star forward wiggled and snaked, red-faced Hildy was right beside him. Six times during the game, Hildy managed to leave the tall, confused boy dribbling nothing but air. And every time she did, she threw the stolen basketball to Nelson.

The pink super sneakers didn't fail Nelson or his team. Whenever Hildy passed him the ball, Nelson made a basket. With lightning speed, his pink feet zigzagged through the High Steppers, then leaped into the air under the basket. As the crowd hushed in amazement, Nelson dropped the ball through the hoop and the Upper Valley squad scored another pair of points. At the end of the game, they were winners by twelve points, and Nelson knew a lot of the credit belonged to Hildy.

"Great game, Crosser," he panted, as their grateful coach threw his arms around Nelson.

"Thanks." The plump girl beamed. "We make a good team, Nelson."

"You bet," answered Nelson, "and from now on, we're *both* starters!" And they were. They practiced plays three days a week at Hildy's house because she had a net over her garage. Together they kept their team on the winning side of every game, so that when the season ended, Upper Valley Station enjoyed an unprecedented 14–0 record. Hildy and Nelson sat on each side of the coach at the basketball banquet held at Martha Sweeney's uncle's restaurant with the marble fountain outside. Before his long speech, Coach Liggit shook Nelson's hand and hugged Hildy. At the end of his long speech, he shook Hildy's hand and hugged Nelson.

"You look different, Crosser," Nelson told Hildy, who was all dressed up in a pink, ruffled skirt and a white blouse with gold buttons. Every time she took a bite of roast beef, she checked to make sure her napkin was tucked in her collar. Nelson, who left his napkin under his plate, ate all his meat, mashed potatoes, and string beans. But he hid the little white dish of beets behind his water glass.

"I *feel* different, too, Nelson," Hildy told him. "I feel *rotten!*"

"Did you eat the beets?" Nelson wondered.

"It's not that," confessed Hildy. "It's just that I'm going to miss being part of a team now that the season's over." His friend looked as if she were about to cry. "Nobody in class made fun of me all winter. Some of the boys even asked me to play ball at recess." Hildy pulled her napkin from under her chin and used it to make a tent over her dish of chocolate pudding. "Now things will go back to normal, and they'll start calling me 'gordo' and 'fatface' again."

"They will not!" insisted Nelson. He remembered how he'd felt when the Weasels laughed at his super pink sneakers. He thought of all the times he'd called Hildy "Old Three Chins" and of how mad she had gotten when David Waldwick made fun of his "Twinkle Toes." "What's so great," he asked her, smiling broadly, "about looking like everyone else anyway?"

Hildy looked doubtful, but she uncovered her pudding. "Besides," Nelson added, "no one will dare tease one of the best players on Upper Valley Station's undefeated baseball team."

"Gee," said Hildy, her round face brightening, "I *was* thinking of trying out for baseball. But how do you know we'll win every game?"

Nelson looked down at his feet. The pink sneakers still fit perfectly, with what seemed like just the right amount of growing room in the toes. The red laces hugged his ankles and the crimson stars blazed on his heels. "Because," he told his friend, "*I'm* going out for the team, too!"

Captain Cavity

But spring came and baseball season started—without Nelson Malone. Instead of trying out for first base, Nelson had decided to concentrate on being undisputed video champ of Upper Valley Station, New Jersey. His pink sneakers lay, dusty and forgotten, under his bed. Every day, as soon as Miss Benito dismissed her fifth-grade class, Nelson rushed home to practice with his television game cartridges. He didn't stop to play kickball at Harry Watson's house anymore. He didn't hang around Matt Hooper's father's gas station to watch them take apart engines. And, although he sometimes brought his mitt to school to throw grounders and flies with the guys at recess, he never went to baseball practice.

Baseball hadn't changed, but Nelson had. After controlling entire armies of video tanks that blazed green fire from their robot turrets, or destroying whole civilizations on alien video worlds, Nelson just couldn't get very excited about an old-fashioned home run. Next to the heady thrill of watching your name blink into electronic life as the high scorer on every arcade game in town, the cheers of a few baseball fans seemed long ago and far away.

"Please, Nelson," Eric begged him. "You've got to come out for the team. You could be the greatest first baseman the Valley Tigers ever had." Eric was still Nelson's best friend, and they still traded lunches, but Nelson didn't have much time to play after school anymore.

"Sorry, Eric," he always told his friend. "I have to get home and practice Space Challenger. I almost broke 3,000,000 yesterday."

"Nelson Malone!" Hildy Crosser scolded him. "I lost six pounds just so we could help the Tigers go undefeated this year." Hildy, who hadn't forgotten Nelson's promise at the basketball banquet, wanted to be the fastest shortstop she could, even if it meant trading all her malted Mini-Milks for carrot sticks. "You said we'd be teammates again."

"Sorry, Crosser," Nelson told Hildy. "I haven't got time for baseball. Besides, I can't risk a hand injury." It was true. Nelson didn't have time for baseball or promises or best friends anymore. In fact, he didn't have time for anything except video games.

Soon Nelson was a better video player than anyone he knew. He was better than Harry Watson, who had scored only 23,450 on the Star Game machine at the bowling alley. He was better than Matt Hooper, who had gotten his initials up just once for high score on the Space Emperor game at Gino of Genoa's Pizza Palace. And when James Decatur, the smartest boy in school, came to Nelson's house to play Counterattack, he had to wait so long for his turn that he got bored and went home.

Success has its price, and Nelson paid it every day. As soon as school was over, he bolted down the basement stairs to his family's recreation room and turned on the television set. He didn't even check the refrigerator to see if Robin had beaten him to the Chocolate Winkies. He didn't even tell his mother about the excellent black eye he'd given Warren Lansdorf at recess or the terrific nosebleed Sheryll Leeds had given herself by holding her breath in music class. Instead he sat hunched over his video console, sharpening his electronic skills until bedtime.

From three o'clock until four, while Robin did her homework, Nelson defended Earth against the relentless laser attacks of alien invaders from planet Ohm. "You're going to be in big trouble when Miss Benito finds out you haven't done your homework," Robin would yell from upstairs.

"I don't care, wo-fat!" Nelson would yell from downstairs.

From four o'clock until five, while Robin and his mother worked on their giant cookie puzzle, Nelson guided yellow Munchies through intricate mazes, helping them to devour blue Meanies, pink Dwarves, and electronic reactivators. "We need help finding the chocolate chips," Mrs. Malone would call down to the basement.

"Maybe tomorrow," Nelson always told her. "Right now I only need two more reactivators to get another game."

When Nelson's father came home, he was always surprised to find that Nelson had spent more time studying the TV screen than his math or spelling assignments. "I don't know why they call it 'home-work,'" Nelson told him. "I finished mine at *school*."

"All of it?" asked Mr. Malone.

"Almost," answered Nelson.

At dinner, the Malones finally stopped asking "Where's Nelson?" They knew he was in the basement, a fork in one hand and a joystick in the other. Without spilling a drop of spaghetti sauce, Nelson could eat dinner at the same time that he drove the full length of the ruinous Death Valley Raceway, avoiding oil spills, wrecked drivers, and pulsating Purple Zoomers. His high score was 285,349,102. That was better than the combined scores of Harold Farlowe, Tom Craig, and Michael Mason, who was a seventh grader.

Just before bed, while Robin was reading the latest adventure of Mindy and Mark Marvel, sister and brother detectives, Nelson would confront his most challenging video opponent—the insidious Captain Cavity. Plaque Patrol was the newest cartridge in Nelson's collection, and it involved the strangest, most complicated program he had ever played.

The commercial that had convinced him to trade his Easter basket for the game featured a huge set of teeth that chomped and chewed and talked all by themselves. "Plaque Patrol," the teeth said, "is not

like any other video game. Once you've been bitten, you won't be able to stop!" The teeth opened very wide and chuckled loudly at their joke. "As Commander of the Plaque Patrol, your mission is to protect an entire mouthful of healthy white teeth from the menace of Captain Cavity and his squadron of ruthless Decay Demons." When the teeth finished this sentence, Nelson noticed something work its way loose from the back of the gums and clatter like a broken teacup across the screen. It was a small white tooth!

"There isn't a dirty trick," the talking mouth continued, "that the corrupt Captain Cavity won't try." The teeth were chattering now, and the voice sounded husky and frightened. Suddenly two big teeth dropped together from the upper jaw, leaving a gaping hole in the front of the mouth. Like the first tooth, they rolled with a sickening clatter and disappeared from the screen. "Decay must be stopped," lisped the frantic voice, "don't let it reach the baby teeth!"

Soon teeth were falling like rain from the pink gums and the clattering sound grew louder as they dropped and rolled across the television screen. "Hurry!" whispered the mouth, its forlorn, flapping gums nearly empty now. "Man the molars! Brush those bicuspids!" At last, only a single, tiny tooth gleamed from the back of the gums. "Irrigate the incisor!" pleaded the desperate voice. Finally, as the last tooth tinkled from the mouth, its toothless jaws clamped shut and stopped moving. There was complete silence, and only the name of the company that made Plaque Patrol and a list of stores that sold it remained on the screen.

Wow! Nelson thought each time he saw the commercial. That's better than Dinosaur's Revenge! And so he had finally told his mother that he would rather have the new cartridge than an Easter basket. Mrs. Malone had been very disappointed. She loved filling Easter baskets with nougat chickens and milk chocolate rabbits. Ever since he had been little, she had packed Nelson's basket with tiny, silly toys—like snap-together models that were too easy or repeat-fire water pistols that he couldn't shoot Robin with because she always told.

"Easter lasts only one day," he told his mother. "Dental hygiene is forever."

Plaque Patrol required more practice than any of his other cartridges. Nelson sat hour after hour until his fingers got numb on the joysticks. He studied the path that ran beside the winding Root Canal to the Baby Tooth Nursery. He practiced maneuvering his army of silver toothbrushes until he could drop a protective shield over a tooth in a matter of seconds. Over and over he plotted his course, perfecting twists and turns to escape the deadly rays emanating from the giant Black Hole, where Captain Cavity and his fiendish Decay Demons were headquartered. But the more Nelson practiced Plaque Patrol, the more discouraged he became.

Never had he faced such an opponent! The cleverness of his arch computer rival, Captain Cavity, was overwhelming. No matter how expertly he dodged and darted, no matter how lightning-quick his reflexes, Nelson was always defeated by the squadrons of round Decay Demons that attacked his Plaque Patrol at every turn. They came at him continually—large, chocolate-covered wafers that could blow up as many as three toothbrushes with a single laser blast from their rich, shiny centers. Then, when a baby tooth's protective shield had dissolved, a heartless Demon would replace it with a smooth sugar coating that meant certain doom. Even if Nelson managed to destroy the villain with fluoride flak from his forward bristles, the little sugar-coated tooth was soon filled with black holes that grew larger and larger until the tooth lost its hold and fell with an empty clatter across the screen and out of the picture.

"Telephone for you, dumbhead," Robin yelled down the stairs in the middle of one of his most challenging battles with Captain Cavity. "It's Eric."

Until now Nelson had never actually seen Captain Cavity, who was programmed to remain in his Black Hole inside the tower-shaped Sweet Tooth until a player destroyed all the fiendish Decay Demons. Today he felt certain that he was about to face his deadly foe at last. "Tell Eric I'll call him back tomorrow," he yelled to Robin. "Tell him I can't come to the phone now. I only have one toothbrush left."

He guided his last silver toothbrush toward the Sweet Tooth, keeping a watchful eye on the depths of the Black Hole. Then, as he fluoridated the last Decay Demon, Nelson thought he saw something moving in the Hole's center. Suddenly Robin was shouting again from the top of the basement stairs.

"Eric says you can't call him tomorrow. He says the Tigers need you today, because Hildy Crosser sprained her ankle and they're losing 28 to 3 to the Wildcats, and you better come right away or he's taking back his pocketknife."

Nelson thought of the little knife, smooth and shiny, with a silver panther on its wooden case. He thought of catching a high fly at first base just in time to put smart aleck Randy Jenkins out and retire the side. "I can't," he told his sister. "I'm just about to meet Captain Cavity. Once you've been bitten, you can't stop!"

When Nelson turned back to the TV screen, he was astounded to find that the sinister captain had already left his headquarters and was moving steadily toward the last toothbrush. Captain Cavity, Nelson discovered at last, was not chocolate-colored like his army of Decay Demons, but bright yellow with a white top. He was shaped like an ice cream cone and kept shooting rays from the long, trembling point on which he glided across the screen.

Clutching the controls, Nelson waited in the dark for the enemy to launch his offensive. Though his fingers itched to push his attack button, it was not until the captain had shot five rays that missed his dodging toothbrush that Nelson was ready to act. Each time the captain blasted a ray from his slender base, a red dot was exposed in the cone's center. Now, guessing that this tiny dot might be the key to Cavity's destruction, Nelson took careful aim and fired a fluoride flare.

Suddenly the ice cream cone quivered, then exploded and disappeared. Nelson watched, fascinated,

73

as the entire television screen became a smoky blur that covered the Nursery, the Root Canal, and the captain's night-black headquarters. But the smoke did not stop at the edge of the screen; it began to billow and puff and fill up the whole recreation room! Nelson could see that the couch, the walls, and even his *Space Aliens* T-shirt had turned dark gray and that the air itself was twisting and curling into billowy clouds.

As the dark smoke filled the room, Nelson heard a horrible sound like the *chomp-chomp-chomp*ing of giant teeth. It grew louder and louder until it seemed to swallow the whole basement. Nelson covered his ears with his hands, then noticed something incredible. The silver toothbrushes and chocolate Decay Demons had left the TV screen and were gliding slowly toward him! The thin silver toothbrushes that he had spent so many hours steering around the video field were now actually pouring out of the television set in a pulsating parade that came to rest in a circle around him. Their bristles rustled as the bright shapes brushed past Nelson and then surrounded him, floating weightlessly a few feet off the ground. Their pink tips trembled softly as they each saluted him with a glowing fluoride flare that spiraled silently toward the rec room ceiling.

What surprised Nelson most was to find the defeated Decay Demons, flat as stepped-on bubble gum, obediently forming a second, larger circle around his toothbrushes. Instead of attacking the toothbrushes with their chocolate lasers, the Decay Demons hovered harmlessly behind them, emitting a high-pitched, squeaky sound, as if twenty-three invisible

blackboards were being scraped by twenty-three invisible chalks. Nelson felt uneasy and expectant but not afraid. He knew this game wasn't over yet!

Then the thing that Nelson had been waiting for happened. Captain Cavity materialized beside him in the center of the double rings. Nelson was not at all intimidated by his cone-shaped rival, because the captain was no bigger than a baseball and his soft ice cream top was running down his slanted sides. The red oval in his middle shone like an angry eye. Now the sound of chomping teeth grew louder than ever, and Nelson held his ears tighter still.

"You have won," someone said in a thin whine that Nelson could barely hear. He uncovered his ears and the mechanical sound became more distinct. "You are the victor, humanoid," said a voice like a rusty door. Nelson felt fairly certain that it was Captain Cavity who spoke, since his opponent's red eye winked open and closed with every word. "You have defeated me," continued the computer voice, just loud enough to be heard over the chattering teeth. "Your super score has terminated Captain Cavity. Because my attack was powerless against your electronic skill, you will receive the ultimate honor. You will be computed."

"What do you mean?" asked Nelson, who felt very warm in the cloudy smoke and was beginning to wish he had never managed to steer his last toothbrush within firing range of Captain Cavity.

"You will become the new game master. You will not be Nelson Malone. You will be King Video, invincible and preprogrammed."

"Preprogrammed?" Nelson looked past the ring of electronic shapes toward the stairs. He wondered if his parents or sister could hear Captain Cavity or the horrible chomping sound that kept pounding away in the background.

"Yes. Preprogrammed. You will not need to eat or sleep. Your heart will be electronic. You will transmit eternally. Hail to King Video, all-powerful Control Module."

The toothbrushes waved their bristles appreciatively and the fat chocolate wafers squeaked with excitement. "Not need to eat?" Nelson thought of the tiny meatballs his mother always added to her spaghetti sauce.

"You will not require food. You will be energized by activators. Leaving the game will not be necessary. You may choose your color now."

"What color?" Nelson asked, although he had a crawly feeling he knew what the captain meant.

The captain shivered and bounced in the air beside Nelson, then rose several feet until his red eye was just opposite Nelson's gray ones. "You will no longer need a body or clothes to put on it. You will be a video shape. Please select your color now."

"But I don't want to be a color," Nelson protested. "What would Mom and Dad say if I woke up orange? And Robin? Boy, she'd never stop laughing!"

Captain Cavity trembled in the air impatiently. "You will not have a family. You will be joined by computer programs to other command terminals." Nelson's former foe ignored two large drops of vanilla ice cream that fell from the tip of his cone. They landed on the couch and slid like wet paint down one leg onto the floor.

Nelson was sorry he had ever asked for the new cartridge. He was sorry he had ever begged for Plaque Patrol instead of a "baby" basket. He remembered the tiny nougat chickens and the chocolate bunnies with pink icing bows. This year Robin had found four new plastic bracelets in her basket and a wind-up egg that spun around the floor in circles before it hatched six fluffy chicks that shot into the air like yellow popcorn. Nelson knew there was only one thing to do.

"Wait a minute!" he yelled at the shapes quivering around him. "I *didn't* win. I couldn't have gotten the high score because I didn't destroy all the Decay Demons." Nelson turned to face the captain and tried to sound apologetic. "I guess I should have told you right away. Count them for yourself."

Captain Cavity's red eye began to blink furiously. "I cannot make an error. I computed twenty-three Demons destroyed. I am programmed to attack only after the last Decay Demon has been eliminated. I computed twenty-three eliminations."

"Well, compute again," insisted Nelson, his arms folded tightly across his chest. "You'll see, all right; you picked the wrong electronic wizard. I mean I'm good, but I'm not *that* good."

The ring of flattened chocolate wafers closed in against the circle of toothbrushes. Then Captain Cavity's yellow cone-shape floated around the entire outside circle, emitting a low, hollow beep each time it passed one of the flat chocolate discs. After he had traveled once around the circle, the captain began to sputter and clank like a broken vacuum cleaner. "Twenty-two. There are only twenty-two Decay Demons here. I computed twenty-three before. There has been a malfunction. There has been a faulty transmission. There has been a . . ."

"*Mistake*," interrupted Nelson, sounding very relieved and a little smug. "You've made a *mistake*."

For a minute the gray smoke in the room got richer and thicker and burst into a bright, fiery glare that lit up the whole basement. Then the chomping teeth and the high-pitched squeaks began to grow louder and louder until it sounded as if the captain and his chocolate wafers were all screaming at the tops of their electronic lungs. Nelson kept his arms locked across his chest as the computer shapes began to fly around him in wild fits and starts. Even though they were all much smaller than Nelson, their mad rush suddenly frightened him and seemed to make the floor he stood on shake.

Just when he was sure he couldn't stand the noise or light any longer, Nelson noticed something peculiar. Behind the squeaks, he could no longer hear the teeth chattering. For one terrifying instant, it was so quiet that Nelson wondered if his own heart had stopped beating. Then, much more suddenly than they had appeared, all the video shapes vanished. The room was dark except for a faint glow on the TV screen.

Only after he had turned off the television set and unplugged his game console did Nelson Malone begin to smile. Then, cautiously, he reached into the pocket of his *Space Aliens* T-shirt and took out a crumpled brown disc with a shiny, dark center. It was flat as an empty balloon, but it let out a tiny, indignant squeak. Nelson grinned sheepishly.

"No hard feelings," he told the twenty-third Decay Demon. "But if I hadn't stuffed you into my pocket, I'd be playing Plaque Patrol for the rest of my electronic life. Besides, I think you'd make a great pocket watch. I'm going to teach you to beep on the hour!"

He dropped the small chocolate-colored wafer back into his pocket and clambered up the stairs out of the basement. He burst into the living room just as his father was fitting a piece into the giant cookie puzzle. His mother and sister looked up in surprise. "Nelson," Mrs. Malone observed, "you've gotten taller."

Nelson noticed that the room looked new, the way things do when you've been away for a long time and then come back. "I thought you might need some help with the chocolate chips," he said, blinking at his family in the bright light. Then he remembered Eric. He rushed to the phone and dialed his best friend's number. "Hi," he said when Eric answered. "Tell the guys that 28 to 3 isn't so bad. Wait till you see how we're going to cream those Wildcats next week!"

The Man
from Mush-Nut

One afternoon, as Nelson dropped his backpack on the couch and raced into the kitchen, he was greeted by the aroma of something that definitely didn't smell like an after-school snack.

Nelson's mother was standing by the refrigerator, holding her nose with one hand and taking everything from the top shelf with the other. "Baybe," she gasped, "we'd better bake reservations at Gino's of Genoa todight."

"What happened?" asked Nelson, backing away from the refrigerator and sending a bottle of Diet Dream French dressing rolling across the floor toward a picnic cooler full of melting butter and soupy ice cream bars.

"I don't dow," answered Mrs. Malone, spraying the bottom shelf with Sparkle-Brite. "But whoeber planted this stink bomb id our refrigerator definitely didn't want us to eat at homb todight!"

"Uh-oh," said Nelson quietly.

"Speak ub," said his mother. "I can't hear you whed I'm holding by dose."

"I don't think," he told her a little more loudly, "that it's a stink bomb. I think it's Mrs. Lerner's Hawaiian Medley." There was something familiar about the horrible smell. "I hid it behind the taco sauce last week."

Nelson's mother stopped holding her nose and looked confused. "I didn't know the Lerners had been to Hawaii," she said.

"I don't think they have," Nelson told her. "It's just that Eric loves tuna fish, so I always trade him your Tuna Surprise for his mom's Hawaiian Medley at lunchtime."

"But that's the healthiest lunch I make you." Mrs. Malone sank wearily onto the step stool she always used to reach the shelves above the sink. "I put everything into that sandwich—wheat germ, bean sprouts, sometimes even artichoke hearts!"

"I know." Nelson felt guilty but a little relieved now that his secret was out. "The truth is, Mom, I'm not really that crazy about surprises."

"I see." His mother sighed. "You prefer medleys."

"No," insisted Nelson. "In fact, I've never even tasted one. They always have green things in them, and they wiggle when you try to get your spoon in. It's just that Mrs. Lerner always puts a Mush-Nut bar in Eric's bag when she fixes him a medley. That's why I trade."

"A Bush-Dut bar?" Mrs. Malone looked doubtful and

was holding her nose again. "What's a Bush-Dut bar?"

"It's just the greatest candy bar that's ever been made, that's all." Nelson tried to think of a way to describe the delicious tingle that his favorite candy always made in his mouth just before he swallowed it. "It's the only peanut bar with a chewy mushroom center," he told her, quoting the slogan he'd seen on a Mush-Nut wrapper.

His mother, who was now reaching into the depths of the refrigerator, feeling for Mrs. Lerner's Hawaiian Medley, sneezed. "What kind of a center, dear?"

"Mushroom," Nelson repeated. "It's the only peanut bar with a chewy mushroom center. It's the best candy bar in the world and, now that the five-and-dime doesn't carry them anymore, Eric's mom is the only one in town who stocks Mush-Nuts." Nelson stared at the half of his mother that wasn't in the refrigerator and hoped she understood. "Mrs. Lerner bought twenty bags on sale for Halloween, but no trick-or-treaters wanted them. Except one little girl, who brought hers back the next day for an exchange."

"An exchange?" Nelson's mother's voice came from under the freezer now.

"Yep. She paid Mrs. Lerner twenty-five cents in exchange for taking back the Mush-Nut bar."

"But you *hate* bushrooms." His mother backed out from the refrigerator with a plastic bowl full of something green that ran down the sides of the bowl and smelled horrible. "All dormal, right-thinking children hate bushrooms."

Nelson held *his* nose now. "Dot the way the Bush-Dut company bakes them, I don't," he explained.

"They're crunchy and terrific, and I wrote them about the five-and-dime, but they deber wrote be back."

Nelson was used to people not writing him back—people like his basketball idol, Mohammed El-Janrez; or the President of the United States, to whom Nelson had sent a money-saving proposal for closing schools after lunch; or the foreign pen pal from Sri Lanka, whose name and address his teacher had given him and who never told Nelson whether he liked the picture of his skateboard.

That's why Nelson, instead of waiting for an answer from the Mush-Nut company, continued to trade lunches with his best friend. And that's why he was very surprised to come home from school one day and find a man from Mush-Nut in his very own living room!

"Hi, there, young fellow," the Mush-Nut man said in one of those loud voices people use when they're trying to treat kids like grown-ups, only everyone knows they don't really mean it. "I hear you've run out of Mush-Nut bars."

"That's right," Nelson told him. "I wrote you about it last month."

"You sure did," the Mush-Nut man boomed. He had a very long nose, long legs, and eyes that were so tiny you could hardly tell what color they were. "Why, the president of the Mush-Nut company himself read that letter." He stood real close and looked at the top of Nelson's head while he put an arm around his shoulder. "He couldn't believe that anyone liked— What I mean is, he was astounded that an eleven-year-old boy could write such a moving, sincere sales pitch

—er, letter. He insisted I come here in person to deliver Nelson Malone a *free three-years'* supply of Mush-Nut bars."

"Wow!" Nelson stared at the huge cardboard carton behind the Mush-Nut man. Unless they had put in lots of those tiny foam worms that people sometimes pack in boxes to keep breakable things from bumping, there must have been thousands of Mush-Nut bars in the carton. "Is that one a day?"

"No, sir," roared the Mush-Nut man. "That's *six* a day!"

"Wow!"

"And that's not all, son. I've been talking with your mom, here." He turned and smiled at Mrs. Malone, who sat on the couch looking surprised. "We think you'd make a great peer spokesman for Mush-Nut bars."

"What's a peer spokesman?" asked Nelson, who was much more interested in multiplying 365 times 3 times 6 than in what the Mush-Nut man was saying.

"Why, a kid selling to kids, of course. On TV, on radio, everywhere the Mush-Nut message is carried, you'd be carrying it." The Mush-Nut man made his hand into a fist and gave Nelson a fake uppercut to the jaw. "What do you say, kid?"

"The Mush-Nut message?"

"Commercials, Nelson Malone, commercials. We're asking you to go on TV and tell every kid in America how much you like Mush-Nut bars!"

"Wow!" Nelson had just realized that 365 times 3 times 6 is 6,570!

That night after dinner, Nelson and his family discussed the Mush-Nut offer. "I'd be happier," Nelson's father told them, "if the company were offering more cash and less Mush-Nuts."

"Still," his mother observed, "there *will* be enough to start a college fund for Nelson, and he *does* seem to believe in the product."

"I believe, I believe," said Nelson, who had already worked his way through a whole day's worth of Mush-Nut bars.

"But they're the *worst* candy bar in the universe," insisted Robin. "All the kids will laugh at you for advertising candy that tastes worse than chocolate-covered ants!"

"Have you ever tasted a chocolate-covered ant, conehead?" asked Nelson. "If not, I could run out to the backyard and get you a couple of free samples." Nelson noticed the stubborn, stiff way his sister's arms were folded, and the way her chin was so high in the air, she could have been scouting enemy aircraft. "Besides, you're just jealous they didn't give *you* a job on TV."

"Now, Nelson," said his mother, "I'm sure anyone would be glad to have the chance you do." She patted Robin's arm and reached for her hand. "But I think we're all glad it happened to someone in our family. Maybe a little celebrity will rub off on the rest of us."

"I'd rather eat ants without chocolate covers than have to listen to Mr. Big Mouth tell everybody in school tomorrow how great he is," Robin said.

"I tasted a chocolate-covered ant in college once," said Mr. Malone. "It really wasn't too bad if you just shut your eyes and pretended the crunch was almonds."

So it was decided that Nelson would become a peer spokesperson for Mush-Nuts, and even though no one else seemed to like the candy bars, nobody laughed when Nelson told them he was going to be on television. Eric, who had been trading away all his Mush-Nuts to Nelson, was disappointed. "Does this mean I won't get any more Tuna Surprises?" he asked.

"I'm sorry, Eric," Nelson told him. "Now that I'm under contract, I'll probably be eating most of my lunches with stars."

All the other children in Miss Benito's fifth-grade class were very excited. Even James Frackey, who was twice as big as Nelson and a much better fighter, was impressed. "Gee, Malone," James asked Nelson, "do you think you could get Jet Jackson's autograph for me? And could you tell him I watch 'Crime Kickers' every week?"

"I'll see what I can do, Frackey," Nelson told him. "But we get awfully busy on the set. Sometimes we forget about regular people like you."

"Nelson," interrupted Miss Benito, "I'm sure we'd all like to hear about your TV commercials *after* social studies." She began to write page numbers on the blackboard but stopped after only two. "Oh, Nelson," she added in the same sweet voice she used to talk to Agatha Penrose, the smartest girl in class, "if you *should* happen to see Wayne Stark, you might just tell him I've never missed a single episode of 'Doctor Heartthrob.'"

When Nelson found out the Mush-Nut commercials were going to be filmed at a New York advertising agency instead of a Hollywood television studio, he was very disappointed. He was sure he'd never meet Jet Jackson or Wayne Stark or anyone else famous. "It looks like I'm the only star here," he whispered to his mother, as the president of the Mush-Nut company and the director of the Top-Notch Advertising Agency rushed over to greet them. It was the first day of shooting, and Nelson was surprised to see that everyone around him seemed more nervous than he was.

"Well, well, well!" That's all the short, round president of Mush-Nut kept saying. Sometimes he said it loudly, arms folded against his barrel chest. Other times he shook his head and whispered softly to himself, "Well, well, well!"

The director of Top-Notch had a lot more to say. In fact, he didn't stop talking, and all the time he talked, he got redder and redder in the face. First he told Nelson's mother what a fine, upstanding son she had; then he told Nelson what a terrific mother he had. Then he told the cameraman and the scriptwriter and the TV director what a fine commercial this was going to be. While he talked, he kept his arm locked around Nelson's shoulders, as if he thought Nelson might try to run away.

In fact, Nelson had no intention of running away. Because, in addition to talking a lot, the director of Top-Notch kept feeding him Mush-Nut bars. Each time he came to the end of a sentence, and before he started another, the agency man would pull a candy bar out of his pocket and hand it to Nelson.

At first all Nelson had to do was eat Mush-Nuts. He ate them while the cameraman took a color test. He ate them while a man with a microphone got Nelson's voice level in between bites. He chomped and chewed while a red-haired lady painted even more freckles than Nelson already had across his nose. "You can't have too many freckles on television," she told him.

Nelson went right on chewing while the director told him to "just be yourself," to react naturally to anything that happened while they were filming. He was still munching when the cameras started to roll, and he was still chewing when a tall man wearing a lot of makeup walked up to him and yelled in his face, "Say, there, little boy, why do you like those Mush-Nut bars so much?"

"Well," answered Nelson with his mouth full, "I like Mush-Nut bars because they're the most crunchy, delicious candy in the whole world. I mean, they might not be much to look at, but who wants to stare at a Mush-Nut when you could be eating it?"

"Aaaa-aa-aah," sighed the director of Top-Notch, smiling and looking a little less red in the face.

"So natural," purred the TV director. "So unaffected and *so sincere*."

"Well, well, well!" said the president of Mush-Nut.

"What would you do, little boy," continued the tall actor, leaning even closer to Nelson, "if I told you the store in your neighborhood didn't stock Mush-Nut bars anymore?"

The actor had thick, bushy eyebrows that seemed to meet in the middle and form one huge eyebrow across the top of his watery eyes. He had a lot of silver fillings in his mouth, and smelled as if he had taken a bath in cologne. Nelson didn't like him much at all.

Nelson swallowed the last bite of the bar he'd been chewing and pulled another from his pocket. "If you told me I couldn't get any more Mush-Nut bars," he said, "I'd punch you right in the nose!" Then he made a fist with one hand and put it up against the tall actor's upper lip.

"Ooo-oo-ooh." The director of Top-Notch beamed.

"So genuine." The TV director applauded. "So unpretentious, so *real*!"

"Well, well, well!" The president of Mush-Nut nodded.

"Ha! Ha! Ha!" laughed the actor in a big, deep voice. "You certainly *do* like Mush-Nut bars, little boy. Just what would you give me for this Mush-Nut I have in my pocket?" He pulled a bar from the pocket of his plaid jacket and waved it under Nelson's nose.

Nelson was about to say that he didn't need to give the man anything, because he had a three-years' supply of Mush-Nuts at home. But he knew that answer wouldn't make a very good commercial, so he put his head in his hands and tried to think of what he would really be willing to trade for the last Mush-Nut bar in the world.

"I'd give you," Nelson decided, scratching his left ear, "three rides on my skateboard . . ."

"Touching!" approved the agency director. "But don't scratch on camera, Nelson."

". . . my mother's Tuna Surprise . . ." added Nelson, scratching his right ear.

"Inspired!" sighed the TV director. "Just stop scratching, son."

". . . and," continued Nelson, scratching his forehead and a tiny red spot under his nose, "my complete collection of Demonic Duo comics, including the one where they made a mistake and put Super Sleuth's head on Horrible Harry's body!"

"Well, well, well!" said the president of Mush-Nut. "Why is the boy scratching so much?"

"I guess he's just nervous, T.S.," the Top-Notch director assured his client. "After all, it's not every day a youngster gets to make a commercial for his favorite candy."

"Or work with a famous actor," added the tall actor, patting Nelson's head.

Nelson, who was now scratching both ears at once while trying to reach another red spot on his chin, didn't say anything.

"Don't worry, everyone," announced the TV director. "We'll just shoot that last sequence over as soon as he stops scratching."

And so they waited. The TV director and the Top-Notch director paced back and forth, while the president of Mush-Nut tried to get the recipe for Tuna Surprise from Nelson's mother. But Mrs. Malone was much too worried about Nelson to pay any attention at all.

"Oh, Nelson, you have little red dots all over your face!" She pushed aside the tall actor and felt Nelson's forehead for fever. "You had chicken pox in kindergarten and your measles shots are all up to date. Why are you covered with spots?"

"I don't know," wailed Nelson. He felt awful. The more he scratched, the more he itched, and now it seemed, that there wasn't a space on his arms, face, back, or neck that didn't burn with a fierce, fiery tingle. "Can you reach my back?"

Nelson's mother scratched his back while Nelson scratched his front, and everyone else paced. "We'll have to call a doctor," Mrs. Malone told the Top-Notch director. "The red spots are getting bigger!"

It was true. The tiny scarlet dots were now expanding into fat, cloud-shaped blotches that began to spread across Nelson's face and hands. Nelson, who couldn't scratch and eat at the same time, had thrown away his last candy bar and sat huddled in a miserable ball beside a pile of empty Mush-Nut wrappers.

"Now don't worry, everybody," instructed the Top-Notch director in a very shaky voice. "I'm going to call my personal physician, and he'll have our little star shining again in no time."

But Nelson didn't look very shiny at all. As soon as the doctor arrived, he took one look at Nelson and asked him what he'd been eating. When Nelson waved his hand toward the candy wrappers, the doctor put his stethoscope in his pocket and started writing on his pad. "Severe allergic reaction," he announced, handing a prescription to Mrs. Malone. "Two teaspoons every four hours, plenty of rest, and avoid contact with the allergen."

"Avoid what?" asked Mrs. Malone.

"Keep him away from those candy bars, of course," the doctor said, handing the director of Top-Notch his bill. "He's allergic to them."

"He's WHAT?" asked the Top-Notch director, losing all the red from his face at once.

"Allergic," the doctor said again. "He's allergic to those—"

"—Mush-Nut bars," said the TV director, weeping behind his sunglasses.

"Yes, Mush-Nut bars," repeated the doctor. "He must never eat another; the reaction could be much worse with the next exposure."

"Well, well, well!" said the president of Mush-Nut, looking as green as Mrs. Lerner's Hawaiian Medley.

Nelson was too busy scratching to be disappointed. At home, his mother put him to bed and fussed over him. When the itching finally stopped, he got ice cream, comic books, and lots of hugs. That night, when his father came home, Nelson told him that his career as a Mush-Nut television spokesperson had ended before it began. Mr. Malone was very understanding. "Well, Nelson," he said, smiling, "if you had to be allergic to something, it's convenient that it's something nobody in town will sell."

"Not in *any* town, Dad," Nelson told his father. "The president of Mush-Nut said I was his last hope and that if I couldn't inject new life into the Mush-Nut company's advertising campaign, he was going to stop making candy bars and go back into his old business."

"What was that?" asked Mr. Malone.

"Dog food," said Nelson. "I told him he should get a very hairy sheepdog for his new spokesperson. That way, if it breaks out in red spots, no one will notice."

But Nelson's sister was not as understanding as his mother and father. "Nelson Malone!" Robin shrieked when she heard the news. "Here I told everyone that my brother was going to be famous, and now look at you—you have spots all over, and you didn't bring back a single autograph!"

"That's where you're wrong, el nerdo," said Nelson. "In fact, I worked with a very famous actor today, and he gave me this for you." Nelson took a small piece of paper from his pajama pocket, unfolded it, and handed it to his sister.

" 'To Robin Malone,' " Robin read out loud. " 'With best wishes from your friend, Wayne Stark.' "

Robin closed her eyes and pressed the piece of paper against her chest. "Wayne Stark, Doctor Heart-throb!" She sighed. "Oh, Nelson, I can't believe Wayne Stark's hand actually held the pen that actually touched the paper and actually wrote my very own actual name!" His sister looked as if she were in a trance. "How can I ever repay you?" she asked.

Nelson shrugged. "That's OK. Just don't ask me to make a commercial with him again." He remembered the smell of the tall actor's cologne in his face. "And don't tell Miss Benito I gave you that autograph, or I'll have to stay after school for a week!"

Nam Ton

The last day of school was usually Nelson Malone's favorite day in the year. But not this year. This year his parents had decided that he was old enough for sleepaway camp. Nelson wasn't so sure.

"It's called Camp Starbright for Boys," he told Eric. "My father was a counselor there when he was sixteen. We all went to see a slide show on camp activities last weekend. Every time the picture changed, Dad stood up and started singing 'Shine on, Sunny Starbright.' It was pretty embarrassing."

Eric, who had been going to overnight camp since he was six, tried to make Nelson feel better. "Camp's not too bad," he said. "At Camp Tall Oaks, the food is really great, and we have a powwow cookout every Friday night." Eric counted on his stubby fingers till he ended up on the one with a Band-Aid. "So far I've been on seventeen powwows. When I've done twenty, I get a pioneer kit with binoculars and a can opener that clips on your belt."

Nelson wasn't convinced. "I don't think they have neat stuff like that at Starbright," he told Eric. "I'll bet even Dad wouldn't have fun there anymore. The whole place is under new management, and the director who showed us the slides kept calling it 'the camp of the future.' He had a big mole, and a handshake like a gorilla. What's more, he didn't know anything about baseball. Can you imagine spending the entire summer at a camp run by someone who never heard of Reggie Jackson?"

The more he thought about Camp Starbright and the closer the day to leave home got, the more stubborn and unhappy Nelson became. "I don't want to pack my dumb old trunk," he told his mother, who had laid out all his shirts and shorts in neat piles on his bed. She was cutting tiny pieces of cloth from a long roll. Each label she cut off said NELSON MALONE in small red letters.

"My goodness," said his mother, sewing a label on the collar of his kung fu pajamas, "your sister is a whole year younger than you, and *she's* looking forward to camp."

"That's because she saw a slide of a girl in some nutty dance costume, and now she thinks she's going to be starring in ballets all summer. So why can't she go and have a wonderful time at Camp Moonbright for Girls without my having to go and suffer at Camp

Starbright for Boys?" Nelson remembered the picture of the wide lake that separated the girls' camp from the boys'. "We'll never even *see* each other. Why do I have to go at all?"

"Because," said Mrs. Malone in a calm, quiet voice, "your father and I have already decided to sneak away by ourselves this summer, and we want you and Robin to have a special time, too." She bit the thread and tied a knot to secure the last tiny label. "You have to admit it beats having Mrs. Winters watch you for a whole month."

But Nelson wasn't so certain. Mrs. Winters was full of wrinkles and pretty mean, but at least with her he would know what to expect. A week before camp started, he decided to write Mrs. Winters an invitation to spend July at his house, but when he asked his mother whether you spelled *wrinkles* with one *l* or two, she laughed and took the letter away.

All during the long, bumpy bus ride he and Robin and two fat footlockers took to camp, Nelson worried. When they finally arrived and a plump, pretty counselor with braids took Robin's hand, and his sister walked confidently away with her without even looking back, Nelson was more worried. Then when a tall, red-haired counselor shifted Nelson's trunk onto his shoulders and carried it off to Cabin Six, he was more worried still.

All eight boys in the cabin were Nelson's age, and two of them had smuggled Choco-bits inside their neatly folded T-shirts and shorts. A big, heavy boy named Alvin wanted to trade Nelson two baseball cards for the onion and tuna fish sandwich his mother had packed, and Nelson's new bunk mate, a thin, blond boy named Marc Brady, offered him a stick of Pink Popper spearmint. That was when Nelson Malone decided the summer might not be as bad as he had expected.

But he still had his doubts. For one thing, there was something very strange about the red-haired counselor. Not only was Cabin Six's leader extraordinarily tall, he was also the strongest person Nelson had ever seen, including Muscles Manning, the famous wrestler, and James Frackey, who had beaten up Nelson three times. During the first few days of camp, the counselor lifted the boys' heavy trunks with one hand, cleared a campsite by pulling up trees by their stumps, and slung two canoes over his shoulder as easily as if they had been made of paper! "Anybody *that* strong," Nelson whispered to his bunk buddy after lights out, "should be playing fullback for the Dallas Cowboys instead of baby-sitting us!"

Marc, who had the top bunk because he'd gotten to camp first, laughed. "Maybe he just likes the great outdoors."

"Maybe," suggested a new voice, very close to Nelson's ear, "you should both close your eye shields and get some rest." Their counselor had appeared suddenly beside the bunk without making a sound. A huge hand pulled Nelson's blanket gently around his ears and tucked it tightly into the edges of the bed. The red-haired counselor had a peculiar, quiet way of speaking that never sounded angry but always made you obey. Nelson and Marc hardly dared move in their blanket cocoons for the rest of the night.

There were other strange things about their leader that left Nelson and his fellow campers puzzled. They all observed, for example, that his face had an eerie, glow-in-the-dark quality. What Nelson had thought was a bad complexion became hundreds of tiny, shimmering dots at night. But the biggest mystery of all was his name. He called himself Nam Ton, a name that Nelson thought would have been perfect for an Indian chief but didn't suit the pale, green-eyed counselor at all.

Cabin Six began to solve the mystery thanks to James Whitley. James wore glasses and tripped over himself on hikes. One day at lunch, James spilled his whole glass of grape punch in Nelson's lap. "I'm sorry," he told Nelson before he poured himself another punch, missing the glass and soaking the tablecloth under his plate. "I'm afraid my attention was wandering. You see, I've just made a remarkable discovery that should shed considerable light on the origin of our peculiar counselor." James always used more words and took twice as much time to say things as everyone else in the cabin. "Did you ever observe," he asked, pushing his glasses over his pudgy nose, "that Nam Ton spelled backward is Not Man?"

Sometimes the boys in the cabin lost interest before James had finished his long sentences, but this time everyone at the table agreed he had really stumbled onto something.

"Come to think of it," added Nelson's bunk buddy,

Marc, "have you ever seen Nam Ton take off his shoes?"

"That's right!" Nelson forgot how homesick he had planned on being this summer and was suddenly very excited. "He sleeps in those work boots all night long." He lowered his voice to a whisper, even though Nam Ton had told them he was going to the lake. "I'll bet he has hooves or claws instead of toes!"

The others were too scared to laugh at Nelson's suggestion. Not a bad sort of scared, but the kind of secret uneasiness that tells you something thrilling and very different is going to happen. The boys felt there was something mysterious about their counselor, and in fact, about *all* the cabin leaders at Starbright. Some of the staff wore gloves to bed, just as Nam Ton wore his boots; others had strange, star-shaped moles that glowed like neon stickers in the dark; none of the counselors ever ate with the campers, and not one of them seemed to know the first thing about running a camp.

That was why, Nelson told the others, all the boys had arrived by bus. "If any of our parents saw what an inexperienced crew is in charge around here, Starbright would be a ghost camp by now! Whoever heard of camp counselors who can't tie square knots?"

"Or a camp director," Alvin reminded them, "who doesn't know how to put up a tent or start a fire?"

"And don't overlook our swimming instructor," James spoke up again. "For an individual who is supposed to be improving our backstrokes, he is much too afraid of water!" The boys knew it was true. They had all watched Aluben, the hairy waterfront counselor, shudder each morning as he threw the kickboards into the lake. And each of them had seen him draw back in horror whenever a camper dove into the cool water.

"You young persons," he told his swimming classes, "should build a bridge across this place. Then you would not have to stop breathing to reach the other side."

If James Whitley helped Cabin Six piece together the mystery of Camp Starbright, Nelson and Marc Brady actually solved it. During the second week of camp, the boys formed a spy team and began a series of secret missions during arts and crafts. Nelson had already made three birdhouses out of tongue depressors, and Marc was working on his eighth plastic lanyard, when they finally noticed that none of the counselors ever took attendance. Since James had suggested that everyone keep his eyes and ears open, Nelson and Marc crept away from the craft house every afternoon to explore, prowl, and get to the bottom of things.

Their last and most exciting mission took them down the winding trail that ran between the lake and dining hall. They had just discovered a suspicious footprint when Nam Ton and the canoeing counselor came striding briskly down the path. The two men were arguing so fiercely that they never noticed the boys scuttle into the bushes ahead of them.

"You must be *belox*!" roared the canoeing counselor in Nam Ton's ear as they rushed along the narrow

trail. "You can't take them *all* back to Voltar. The laboratory only needs to study *one*."

"Hear me, Tibro," Nam Ton answered in a voice lower and less harsh than his companion's. "They are good specimens. I have become quite fond of them, and they are all so different." He looked toward the bushes where the boys, as if on signal, ducked lower and held their breath. "How can you choose just one typical Earth type? Which one would you choose?"

Tibro's face was puffed and red. "It doesn't matter which one we take," he insisted. "Our mission is to collect specimens, not befriend them. Mine are dangerous. They were *grotty* enough to find my transmitter, and if this keeps up, they could figure out that it is not a simple Earth radio. Worse yet, they may uncover the transporter."

"That just shows what intelligent samples they are," Nam Ton declared. "Did you know they can make a most *fexy* sound with their mouths and on their radios? They call it 'music.'"

"I call it 'a mistake,'" concluded Tibro grouchily. "But we will ask the director. He must decide how many of these Earthlings should return with us."

As soon as the two counselors had walked away toward the director's office, Nelson and Marc hugged each other in delight. "Space creatures!" they squealed, as happy as if they had both won giant TV screens and a lifetime supply of video tapes.

"Real men from outer space!" yelled Marc, leaping up and down in the middle of the trail and destroying the mysterious footprint. "That's why they never eat!

That's why they don't know anything they should. Nelson, our counselors are *aliens*!"

"I'll bet," said Nelson, thinking of his friend Eric at Camp Tall Oaks, "that we're the only kids in the world with extraterrestrial counselors!"

Sharing a camp with spacemen was a heavy responsibility. Nelson and Marc decided to call all the cabins together to discuss their discovery. That night, while their strange counselors gathered to plan the next day's schedule, the campers of Starbright held a secret meeting of their own. It turned out that Cabin Six was not the only group to have been suspicious of the camp's staff. Everyone, from the shrimps in Cabin One to the seniors in Seven and Eight, had strange facts to report. But it was Nelson and his friend who had actual proof that Camp Starbright was about to become the most exciting place they had ever been!

The one person who wasn't especially pleased with their news was the boy who had started it all. "I think we should tell the authorities immediately," James Whitley said with a frighteningly grown-up frown. "This could be a very dangerous situation. They obviously intend to kidnap one of us. Perhaps even more than one."

"I hope it's *more*," said Nelson. "If I have to make another birdhouse, I'm going to go nuts!"

"Me, too," added one of the seniors. "Here we've got a chance for the best summer of our lives, and *you* want to blow the whistle on them!" He glared at James as if the younger boy had just suggested keeping school open all year long.

"That's right," another boy told James. "Haven't you seen enough movies about aliens to know the one thing we *shouldn't* do is let the grown-ups in on this?"

James looked doubtful, but Nelson knew the others were right. "In the movies, every time the police or anyone in authority learns about space creatures," he told his cabin mate, "it spells doom. Either the space creatures get scared and blow up the town, or the army gets scared and blows up the space creatures. Either way, it's the end of the movie!"

James finally agreed to keep the secret. In fact, when he thought about archery lessons, he realized that traveling to another planet might be better than staying at camp. Even with his thick glasses, he could barely see the target. All the boys laughed when his arrows landed in tree trunks, in cabin doors, and once, in Henry Gressler's egg-salad sandwich. The more he considered things, then, the more James thought he might like being an interplanetary specimen. But he had no intention of visiting Voltar alone. "I have a proposal," he said, pushing his glasses up toward his eyebrows. "Why don't we tell the aliens that we will divulge their existence unless they agree to take the entire camp to their planet?"

Nelson saw the beauty of James's plan before the other boys did. "It's perfect!" he yelled. "All or none. The spacemen will have to take us all, or the rest will tell." Everyone in the group of campers watched him expectantly, waiting for him to explain. "And they'll have to bring us all back, too! Don't you see?" he asked. "You can't just wipe out a whole camp without giving yourself away! If they don't want Earth to know they're here, they're going to have to do things *our* way!"

Nelson Malone was right. Noom, the camp director, knew it. He rubbed one gloved hand thoughtfully over the purple mole by his nose and decided that the two boys in his office were smarter than they looked. Nelson and James had been chosen to represent the campers and present their demands to the director. The plump spaceman hesitated only a moment before shaking hands with the boys. "Done!" he announced. "Voltar will receive you all. The campers will be teleported this afternoon. We will return you within two Earth weeks."

It was decided that before he left, each boy would write five letters to his parents so his family wouldn't worry. Once the letters had been written and mailed, everyone lined up behind Noom and Nam Ton. All the campers carried items their extraterrestrial hosts had asked them to take to the Voltar scientists for further study. Some carried radios; others, video games or goldfish swimming in plastic bread bags. Nelson took three of his mother's walnut brownies in a round red can.

The trip through space to Voltar was not as exciting as Nelson had hoped. The hidden transporter turned out to be not a flying saucer or rocket ship, but merely a single control panel hidden under a rock by the archery range. One by one the boys stepped in front of the panel while Noom pushed its activator button and announced their destination—the planet Voltar in the galaxy Hibernia. The panel converted each boy's body into an energy current, which was sent like a telegram to the hilly purple shores of a pink lake trillions of light-years from Earth.

The pink water looked very inviting. Nelson, who still hadn't learned to do the breaststroke but always won crawl relays, was the first to reach the lake's edge. Just as he was about to stick his foot in the current, Nam Ton raced to his side, shouting and waving frantically. "Stop, stop, my young friend! This swamp is not what it appears to be." Marc Brady and one of the senior boys started to dabble their fingers in the thick pink liquid, but Nam Ton stopped them, too. "This is not water," he told them. "Look closely, but do not touch."

The boys peered cautiously into the lake's depths, stooping down to inspect what seemed to be a whirling, rosy current. To their amazement, they saw not water but thousands of tiny pink animals wiggling and curling around each other in endless, frantic waves. There were so many of the tiny creatures and they were so closely packed together, that from a distance they had seemed to form a single large body of water.

"They're alive!" yelled Nelson, pulling his toes back from the pink mass. "And they have teeth! What are they, Nam Ton?"

"They are called *'zeentex,'*" their counselor told the boys. "There are too many of them to count. Their bite is not poisonous, but it is permanent. Actually," he explained, "we Voltarians go out of our way to annoy the *zeentex*. Every time we are bitten, we get a new glow patch. The patches help us see at night without a need for lights."

Nelson and the others stared again at the countless *zeentex*. They were shaped like fish, and their sharp white teeth flashed in their pink heads. Although all the boys wanted glow-in-the-dark moles like their counselors, they knew such wonderful souvenirs would give them away back on Earth. Reluctantly they formed a line behind Noom and followed him away from the *zeentex* lake.

During the next two weeks, Nelson spent some part of every day in the sky blue laboratory building, where he and the other boys were gently poked, measured, and even sniffed by Voltarian scientists. The rest of the time, however, it was the campers' turn to poke and inspect. Nam Ton took Cabin Six on daily walks through the capital city of Wob Niar, where creatures wearing light instead of clothes stared at the young Earthlings with great interest. Each day Nelson and the others learned new, incredible things about their friendly hosts. Once, when Nam Ton had forgotten to tell a family that they were coming, the boys found the mother, father, and two baby Voltarians still sound asleep, hanging upside down like bats from their ceiling! The campers discovered that no one on Voltar ate more than once a year. The aliens used their mouths to smile large Voltarian grins, but their teeth were striped and hollow, good not for chewing but for storing tiny food pellets that took months to dissolve and helped the space people grow as strong and tall as comic-book heroes.

It was because of his mother's brownies that Nelson Malone had a more exciting adventure on Voltar than any of the other campers. It was on the next-to-the-last day of their stay that the laboratory scientists finally began to study Nelson's can of brownies. They became so interested in the dark, slightly stale cakes that they kept Nelson in the glass examination room long after the other boys had returned to the cluster of gold guest houses that had been assigned to them.

"These squares smell very *serrt*," one bald scientist told Nelson, "but when I try to string one on my necklace, it falls apart. How can you enjoy them if you do not wear them by your nose?"

"Smelling isn't the best part of brownies," Nelson told the tall elderly man. "Eating is." Nelson chomped slowly on one of the brownies to demonstrate, while the wrinkled scientist and five associates watched in fascination. After the brownie was eaten, Nelson had a terrible time explaining to the team of scientists why he couldn't bring it back again. When the last brownie had disappeared in the same way and not a single crumb was left to analyze, Nelson was at last free to join the other boys.

But he had forgotten the way back to the guest houses! He had always been with the rest, and now, no matter which way he turned, he was confronted by a maze of green streets that all looked identical. He finally struck off from the laboratory in a direction he hoped would bring him to the gold domes. He followed the road he'd chosen until it came to a bridge that spanned the pink *zeentex* lake.

Although the bridge didn't feel too sturdy, Nelson decided to chance crossing the swirling lake as quickly as possible. It was not until he was halfway across that the bridge began to crumble beneath him, and Nelson became truly frightened. Like the rabbit he had once surprised in the beam of his flashlight, he was too scared to move. As the ancient footpath sank closer and closer to the sea of shining white teeth, Nelson stood frozen, unable to go forward or back. Instead, he yelled as long and as loud as he could.

Suddenly he saw something approaching at great speed. It appeared to be a man flying rapidly toward him over the pink lake. As the figure neared, Nelson was astounded to see that it was Nam Ton! His counselor had removed the striped footcovers he had worn since they arrived on Voltar, and the reason he had always worn boots on Earth was now clear. For Nam Ton had, to Nelson's amazement, neither hooves nor claws, but a pair of the most bright, beautiful wings that Nelson had ever seen, sprouting from his ankles!

"Hold tight, my friend." Nam Ton hovered overhead, scooping one strong arm around Nelson's waist. Just as the bridge collapsed, Nelson's left foot touched the *zeentex* lake and he felt a small, sharp tingle on his heel. The next instant he found himself high above the sea of swarming creatures, who were left squabbling over the sneaker they had managed to pull from his foot. Nam Ton and Nelson rose quickly into the sky with the counselor's flaming orange feathers beating

the air behind them. Soaring above the bridge, Nelson heard a soft *plop* as his lost sneaker was sucked underneath the hungry lake.

Soon Nelson forgot all about being scared and watched with delight as the spaceman's winged feet kicked circles of light across the darkening clouds. All six of Voltar's suns were setting, and the path of Nelson and Nam Ton's flight spread out like a trail of glowing sparklers against the sky. Nelson also forgot all about being polite. He couldn't resist reaching down to stroke one of the glowing orange feathers. "Please, stop," begged Nam Ton in the quivering voice that was a Voltarian laugh. "You're tickling me!"

When they landed outside the guest houses, the others all came rushing to meet them. Since their arrival, the boys had seen many of their former counselors without gloves. They had watched their hosts use strange, sticky finger pads to scale the sheer glass cliffs that dotted Voltar. But until now, no one had seen Nam Ton without boots. As they stood in a hushed circle around the tall alien with wings as bright as his hair, they knew now that his was the best secret of all.

"When do the rest of us get a ride?" James finally broke the silence. "And how come Nelson got a glow patch?" As the whole camp pressed around him, Nelson looked down at the heel that had touched the *zeentex* lake. It was true! There on his foot, glowing brightly, was a small blue star! He had never been so proud.

Of course, all the other boys wanted to take off immediately with Nam Ton and get glow patches of their own from the *zeentex.* The counselor told them, however, that too many glow patches would certainly arouse suspicion. For one of them to return home with a single accidental patch was bad enough, he explained, but a whole busload of glowing campers would certainly give the spacemen away. "If you wish to return to Voltar, Nelson must remain the only Earthling with a glowpatch."

And he did. All during the last day on Voltar and the hurried packing at Starbright, Nelson was treated like a hero. Everyone fought over who would sit next to him at meals and on the bus ride home. Over and over, the other boys asked him to pull down his left sock so they could stare at the tiny blue star still shining on his heel. Even though they all desperately wanted their own *zeentex* stars, they comforted themselves with the promise their counselors had made: If every boy at Starbright kept Voltar's secret, the whole camp would be able to return to the planet next summer.

It was a promise Nelson was determined not to see broken. As the bumpy Starbright bus brought him closer and closer to home, he realized how hard it would be not to share his exciting news with his best friend. It wasn't easy to keep things from someone as nosy as Eric, someone who always told Nelson *his* secrets and who always gave Nelson half the butterscotch Ringers in his lunch box.

Keeping secrets from his parents was a problem, too. As soon as he stepped down from the bus, his mother hugged him as if he were a tiny little child who had been lost in a department store. "All those letters! You don't know how worried they made us!" Her eyes looked shiny, as if she were about to cry. "I knew you couldn't possibly be having any fun if you had the time to write home so often!" She helped Nelson with his footlocker while his father went to get Robin and her bulky trunk from the other end of the bus. "It's going to be all right, dear," Mrs. Malone told him. "We'll find a different camp for next year. Or maybe you won't even have to go to camp at all."

Not go back to Starbright! Nelson couldn't believe what he was hearing. "Mom," he insisted, "it was terrific at camp. In fact, it was the best summer I ever had in my whole life!" He watched Robin and his father loading her trunk into the car, wondering miserably if he would ever see Cabin Six or Nam Ton or Voltar again!

Suddenly his sister dropped her end of the heavy metal locker with a thud. She came running over to their mother. "Nelson is absolutely, positively, one hundred and twenty percent right, Mommy," she told Mrs. Malone. She pulled on her mother's hand and looked terribly worried and serious. Nelson, who, according to his sister, had never been right before, was very surprised.

"The summer was wonderful," Robin continued. "Besides, camp is an important experience for growing girls and boys. Both Nelson and I just *have* to go back next year. Don't we, Nelson?"

Nelson Malone stared hard at his sister. In all the excitement at Camp Starbright, he hadn't thought much about the girls at Moonbright. Had their summer been as special as his? Did he have someone to share his secret with after all? "Robin," he asked, looking his sister straight in the eye, "just what *was* Camp Moonbright like, anyway?"

Robin, who was still holding her mother's hand, smiled such a big grin at Nelson that he noticed her new tooth had grown all the way in. He was amazed to see that it didn't look at all like her others. It was round and striped with bright rainbow bands of color. "Camp Moonbright was out of this world, dum-dum," she told him. "Just plain out of this world!"

WORLDS OF WONDER FROM AVON CAMELOT

THE INDIAN IN THE CUPBOARD
60012-9/$2.95US/$3.95Can
THE RETURN OF THE INDIAN
70284-3/$2.95US only

Lynne Reid Banks

"Banks conjures up a story that is both thoughtful and captivating and interweaves the fantasy with care and believability" *Booklist*

THE HUNKY-DORY DAIRY
Anne Lindbergh   70320-3/$2.75US/$3.75Can

"A beguiling fantasy...full of warmth, wit and charm"
Kirkus Reviews

THE MAGIC OF THE GLITS
C.S. Adler   70403-X/$2.50US/$3.50Can

"A truly magical book" *The Reading Teacher*

GOOD-BYE PINK PIG
C.S. Adler   70175-8/$2.50US/$2.95Can

Every fifth grader needs a friend she can count on!

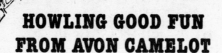

HOWLING GOOD FUN
FROM AVON CAMELOT

Meet the 5th graders of P.S. 13—
the craziest, creepiest kids ever!

M IS FOR MONSTER
                    75423-1/$2.50 US/$3.25 CAN
by Mel Gilden; illustrated by John Pierard

BORN TO HOWL   75425-8/$2.50 US/$3.25 CAN
by Mel Gilden; illustrated by John Pierard

THERE'S A BATWING IN MY
      LUNCHBOX   75426-6/$2.50 US/$3.25 CAN
by Ann Hodgman; illustrated by John Pierard

THE PET OF FRANKENSTEIN
                    75185-2/$2.50 US/$3.25 CAN
by Mel Gilden; illustrated by John Pierard

Buy these books at your local bookstore or use this coupon for ordering:
....
Avon Books, Dept BP, Box 767, Rte 2, Dresden, TN 38225
Please send me the book(s) I have checked above. I am enclosing $_____
(please add $1.00 to cover postage and handling for each book ordered to a maximum of
three dollars). *Send check or money order*—no cash or C.O.D.'s please. Prices and numbers are subject to change without notice. Please allow six to eight weeks for delivery.

Name _____

Address _____

City _____ State/Zip _____

                                        P.S.13 -5/88